UNTAMED

Jillian Dunlay

www.JillianDunlay.com

Prologue

We don't have much time.

The Forces are slowly making their way through each country. Through much bloodshed, they reign victorious, ruling as tyrants in a once democratic land. To see the people of every nation bow down to these persecutors is sickening. They are worse than the Taliban. The situation is beyond help.

You knew this would happen. I can't say I'm surprised; your nation has always had a much more advanced system compared to the others. But now is the time to pursue these advancements.

There aren't many left, you see. About 70 countries remain of the previous 196. Yes, the damage is horrific. But we can savor what is left. I am not letting them destroy every bit of our world. That cannot be done.

You need to begin gathering the offspring which you have prepared for this. They have the power to defeat these tormentors. They are the only ones who have any remote chance. After you inject the Glocylic serum inside them, your captives should be prepared for war. Make sure the regular citizens of your country do not gain knowledge of this. A riot would be caused, and panic would be a disease, slowly spreading amongst your people.

They have found their way to Syria. And I know, soon enough, they will find their way to you.

The once smooth ground is painted with streaks of red. My people, they are terrified, cowering in their homes until one of them breaks in. I can hear their screams building to an echoing screech, until it painfully comes to nothing but a blood-chilling silence. That is when I know another life is taken. That is when I know they have stolen yet another soul. It's as if they enjoy it. How wrong is it that someone can enjoy watching the light die from someone's eyes? How could you ever enjoy taking something so precious as a life? This I do not understand.

I am hoping this letter arrives to you before The Forces do. I am hoping you will make it out alive. I am hoping you will use your strengths to not only help your people, but the remaining people of the world. Hope. A risky word indeed, but you must grasp it, hold it with lust, and not let go.

Sincerest wishes,

Uri Riham

President of Syria

Part One

Platinum

When I open my eyes, the other side of the bed is empty.

My cat, Buttons, is not there to greet me in the warmth of morning, the calico patterns of her fur reflecting the light of dawn. I listen for the familiar clanging of pots and pans as Crimson races down the stairs for his daily breakfast of scrambled eggs, but the clanging never comes. I continue listening intently, desperately searching for the familiarity of Emerald stomping around in her bedroom, complaining how she has nothing to wear even though she's got three closets piled high with clothes.

Instead I am met with cold silence.

It's not the good silence, either. It's not the type that fills you with a sense of calm as if the world has suddenly stopped and for a moment you are trapped in its endless beauty, like the first time you see the leaves change during autumn or how the colors of the rainbow sparkle within every rain drop that hits the ground. No, this is the kind of silence before thunder shakes the universe.

It is not a pleasant silence.

As my eyes finally adjust to my surroundings, the monotonous colors of the walls lure my mind into a state of dreariness. Three solid walls enclose me, each a darkened shade of grey, with the fourth side lined with bars as if it is a jail cell. The bars are fairly close together. Outside there is a hallway, also colored with the same monotone grey. Just the atmosphere alone makes me miss looking at the bright, vintage shops of which I'm used to seeing line the streets.

The next thing I notice is the blood on the floor, and the scratches on the walls. Not common sights in my small town of West Lake, located in northern New York's Hudson Valley, that's for certain. I kneel down onto the hard, metal ground, letting my fingertips run over the blood stains. They aren't new, but certainly not old. I'm not curious as to why the stains are there. I know why. I've been in this place for a mere seven days, but it's not like I don't hear the screams at night.

The screams come in waves. Sometimes I sleep soundly throughout the night, and for those precious hours I pretend Buttons is next to me with her nose pushed up against my cheek, and that Crimson is going to run into my room asking if I want to watch cartoons with him in the middle of the night to help with his nightmares. But then there are the times when I barely have a second to shut my eyes before another scream is released into the dark, and I can't help but wonder when that scream is going to be clawing its way out of my own throat.

"Miss Woods."

I shove my greasy, platinum locks away from my eyes and stand up. One of the guards has approached my cell.

"Your brain scan is scheduled for Wednesday at 3:00 p.m. with Dr. Layenne."

I nod. "That's fine, thank you."

I let my head hang limp as I hear the clacking of his shoes ring in the distance before I climb into my cot. My eyelids are heavy. It's not just my eyelids, though. Everything has felt heavy lately.

As my eyes envelop themselves in darkness, the visions come. I find myself running around a city once more, greeted by masses of corpses with their eyes black and bones broken. I press my ear against the chest of each one, hunting for the slightest heartbeat but finding none. Then the guilt comes, creeping up my back until my spine is snapped from the pressure. That's the worst part. That's always the worst part.

And then I'm no longer dreaming, but wide awake.

"Let me go!" The words try to escape from my mouth, but the guards' hands are shut tight over my mouth. I would use my hands or legs, but they've restrained those as well.

They pin me down into a wheelchair, and I am wheeled against my will into what appears to be a psych ward. The nurses and doctors do an interrogation, and I give them my answers over and over again: I am not having any visions, I have never had any visions, and I am feeling just fine.

Just fine. That's a common answer in this place.

The visions seem to be a popular topic of interest. I'm not sure why, exactly, but in the late afternoon if you eavesdrop just right, you can make out the daily discussions between staff members wandering the halls. It's always something to do with the visions, whether they're good or bad or however they're interpreted. I don't see why they're such a big deal. What a person sees when they close their eyes should be their own concern, nobody else's.

I lie through my teeth with every question they ask: *Are you having visions? Have you ever had visions?* And the worst of all *Do you know why you're here?* No, no, and no. Once they are finished, I'm released back into my cell. I catch whispers of the nurses swearing under their breath, but it's best to ignore it. The patients in this place are treated quite poorly, from what I've observed.

My resistance to the guards is evident on my skin. My wrists and knuckles are swollen, and blood dribbles from the corner of my mouth when I attempt to scream. I am proud of these wounds. It shows that my spirit has not yet been broken by these inhumane superiors.

I swipe at the blood near the corner of my mouth and paint it on the floor next to all the other blood stains. If I die in here, at least I have something to show for it.

***

The wind bites at my knuckles, and for a minute I believe I am free until I realize it was not the wind at all, but instead the gush of air from the opening of the cell door.

"Hello, Platinum." My heart rate rapidly picks up at the sound of Penny's voice, and I am out of bed instantly, throwing my arms around her frail body.

"How are you today, dear?" Penny is maybe the only nurse in the institution who does not treat her patients as if they're prey waiting to be captured. Her kind, warm eyes bestow on me a sense of hope, and I manage to give her a small smile in return.

"I'm fine," I tell her, but the look of sympathy she gives me tells me she knows I'm not.

"Would you like to play cards?" She pulls a deck out of her pocket. The corners are worn and yellowed, and I wonder how many others have touched these cards.

"Sure, that'd be nice." We play several hands of blackjack, and she tells me stories of her childhood that soothe my thoughts for a long while.

"You know, Platinum, when I was a teenager I looked just like you." She grins, the wrinkles on her face becoming even more defined.

"Really?" Her comment amuses me. "You were awkwardly tall with skin as pale as a polar bear's fur?"

Penny chuckles. "Indeed, I was. But even more so, I had a look of adventure."

My eyebrows furrow. "How do I have a look of adventure?"

"You just do. It's a look of wonder, and a look of life. You are going to do something remarkable with your life, Platinum Woods."

I appreciate her kind words, but I can't help but think that I might never have that chance.

"Oh my," Penny looks at her watch sadly. "It seems I'd best be going. Remember, dear, you're always welcome to reach out to me, and I'll be at your aid in a jiffy."

"I know. Thank you, Penny." She gives my hand a light squeeze before she exits, pushing the cell door closed once more.

But the click of the lock never comes.

I know I should say something, anything, but my eyes silently follow her down the hall as she walks away, taking the key with her.

The cell door hangs open, only an inch wide, but an inch nonetheless. It calls to me, tempting my mind with possibilities of freedom and the slightest chance of seeing my family again. As I creep towards the door ever so slowly, the devil on my shoulder hisses a luring melody into my ear. I let it flow through my veins, and it blocks out any resistance I otherwise had.

It takes all the courage in my body to lay my fingers against the cold rust of the handle. Without thinking, I pull, and the hinges rub together as if calling to the guards, "She's escaped!"

There is nothing to do but run.

It takes only seconds before bullets begin soaring past my head. The guards yell for me to stop, and they threaten me with words, but I don't care. Words are just words.

All the hallways look the same. I keep my eyes peeled for a gleaming red exit sign, but everything around me is a monotonous grey. The bullets are coming faster now, and a lot more accurate, with one barely missing the surface of my right cheek. I have no choice but to start ramming into doors to see if any will budge enough to open.

Then one finally does.

When I step outside, a bright flashing light hits me. It is not the light of the sun, basking me in all its glorious freedom, but instead a camera. Not one camera, but dozens of them.

I don't even get a chance to react before a microphone is shoved into my face.

"We're live at the Government Mental Institution," a reporter calls out. "Are you Platinum, the 16-year-old capable of seeing the future?"

Another chimes in, "Platinum, why do you claim that our country is going to fall?"

My mom once told me something my uncle always said: "Fill your eyes to the brim with as much wonder as you can. It is then that you'll see the world for what it truly is, all the beauty, chaos, and everything in between."

But all I see is chaos.

"Get the hell away from me!" I take one of the microphones from the reporters and bash him in the head. News teams back away in shock, and I hear the shatter of a camera as it collides with the cement.

I realize this may be my one opportunity to warn everyone. They don't know of what's to come. I stare into the lenses of the remaining cameras, swallowing my pride as I do so.

"My name is Platinum Woods. For those of you watching, you might just see me as some psycho girl who can't even think straight, and if that's the case, that's fine. Live your lives. But I just want to say this: this country is going to go to shit unless the people being contained here are released. Don't trust whatever these so-called officials are telling you! They're manipulating you into thinking I'm some horrible person, when in reality, I'm the only one who can save you. We are going to die unless we take some sort of action—"

It is at this point that staff members tear me away from the focus of the cameras and pin me to the ground. They try to clean up my mess to the reporters and viewers, explaining that I'm not mentally stable, but they know the truth. They're just afraid to admit it.

As I am led back inside, Penny is standing to the side of the hallway. Out of the corner of my eye, I catch her giving me a wink.

Maybe I do have a look of adventure.

***

From the day we are born, we are given a label.

As we grow older and become enveloped in environments such as public school, we begin to define ourselves with these labels, whether we like it or not. I was always the weird girl. The weird girl with no friends because she was a foot taller than all her classmates, and had skin as pale as a ghost. I never minded much, though. When people would call me weird or different, I'd think to myself, "Thank you for appreciating the fact that I don't dress in shorts that reveal too much skin just like every other girl in our grade." Or if they'd call me a nerd, I'd find it humbling that they believe I'd rather be reading a thoughtful literature classic than obsessing over the latest celebrity break up. It all seems so foolish.

But here, it's different. Here, if you are different, you are killed.

These thoughts cloud my mind as I slowly pace around the cell, boredom filling the passing seconds. I might as well try to break these handcuffs apart. That should make the time go quicker.

Screeching in anger, my hands slam on everything in the room, struggling to make the stubborn chain snap. At least an hour passes. All I manage to do is reopen the wounds on my wrists. As I begin to smash the handcuffs into the metallic surface on the wall, something catches my eye.

My calendar.

I've always been one to keep track of time, as I tend to be somewhat of a perfectionist. When the security guards ordered me to come with them, I quickly ran upstairs and snatched my calendar from the bulletin board in my bedroom before leaving. Underneath the words *December 2032,* I see a day circled with a red felt marker.

Wednesday.

The brain scan.

My nerves scatter, and my pulse beats a thousand times a minute. Not knowing what else to do, I race over to the sink, and struggle to refrain from vomiting.

"Someone help me!" I cry, and lean against the wall, its freezing surface now comforting. Tears slide down my face, stinging my skin as though a razor is slicing through my flesh. My eyes, once an innocent blue, are dark and grey, a brewing storm. My hair, once a silky sheet of snow, is now a tangled white-blonde mop. I feel as though I've already lost myself in just the little time I've spent here.

"Yes. And you have the medications ready?"

A voice, clear as day, drifts through the opening of a vent within my cell. Of course, most wouldn't have the ability to hear a far voice with such clarity, but it's a skill I've always possessed. I discovered it when I was around four years old. I could hear my grandma's dog barking into the night even though she lived several blocks away.

The voice belonged to none other than the president of the United States. I press my body against the vent, and eavesdrop on the conversation.

"Yes, sir. The meds are prepared in the injections. How many do you need?"

I recognize the burly voice as one of the guards.

"I'd say about 200. Those are just for the captives in this local area, though. In total, about 5,000."

What injections?

"Five thousand injections? That's quite a lot, Mr. President. How many people is the government containing? And for what purpose?"

The president sighs sharply. "Do not question my orders. Your job is to make sure the local captives consume the medicine. Do you understand?"

I am a local captive.

"Yes, but isn't this going against the people's rights, sir? You're not possibly going to take their lives, are you?"

"Of course not! Why would you ever form such a senseless idea?"

"My apologies, sir."

Another sigh. "Go, it's your leisure time. Remember, Platinum's brain scan is tomorrow. She's quite a complex human being. If I were you, I'd get all your restraining weapons ready—and don't be afraid to injure her. When she got loose yesterday, I was this close to firing all the guards. To have a danger like her escape one of the country's top mental confinement centers puts a shame on the entire foundation of our government. Not to mention that the national news captured all of it on camera. Are you prepared for tomorrow?"

"Yes, Mr. President." I catch the uncertain waver when the guard speaks.

"Good. You're dismissed."

The guard obediently exits, but I hear the sound of the president's cell phone being used. His voice still echoes throughout the hallway. I stay with my ear pressed against the vent.

"The guards have all fallen for it, so everything's in place. Now, we just must make sure the captives consume the medication, and it will all go according to plan."

Curiosity and bewilderment course through my veins. I press my ear closer to the cell door.

"Yes, she is definitely my largest concern. She's being tested tomorrow. I'll most likely kill her, she's an obvious threat. There's a high probability she knows what we're planning, and considering how defiant she is, she'll figure out a way to damage our operation before it even starts."

I don't even have to question whether or not I'm the topic of discussion.

"Yes, the one who was on television yesterday. Fair skin, long pale blonde hair, and light blue eyes. Sixteen, I assume."

My heart stops.

The president chuckles. "Innocent as she may seem, she's one of the most wanted people in America. There's something going on in her brain, and I'm determined to abolish whatever it is."

Shit.

"Thanks. Good day to you, too."

Firmly, I hear the "end call" button beep. But I'm not a fool.

The president of the United States is a murderer.

And I'm his latest target.

***

I am invincible.

My mother used that word quite often whenever she'd be talking with her sister on the phone. She would say things like, "Oh, you know how teenagers are. Always thinking they're invincible, that they can survive anything that comes their way. Platinum's just going through her teenager phase."

I hated how she put such a negative twist on such an empowering word. The way I see it, anyone can be invincible. It is not about the actual state of invincibility, but instead grasping the hope that you could be, therefore allowing your spirit to take risks and chances; taking those risks and chances is how we are shaped into the people we become. But it seems as you age and mature, your belief in that empowering invincibility grows weak, and you are sucked into the eternal mediocracy of adulthood.

Standing here, with my hands clasped behind my back and sides flanked by nurses, I vow to myself to never lose that sense of invincibility. I'm afraid that if I do, I might not make it out of here alive.

"Miss Woods, are you prepared?" one of the nurses asks, and I nod. They lead me out of my cell into a dimly lit hallway. Hanging onto my newfound threshold of invincibility seems to prove more difficult than I thought. A spiraling pain shoots up my leg like the tip of a spear had immersed itself into my flesh, and I fall to the ground.

"Oh, dear!" One of the nurses crouches down next to me. I don't dare to even glance.

"It seems a nail has punctured your foot. They litter the ground in this place, constantly coming loose from old door hinges. Very sorry about that."

Her oblivious tone infuriates me. "How deep is the cut?" I ask her.

"Fairly deep, unfortunately. I have some gauze that can temporarily stop the blood flow, but it looks like you'll need some stitches. That can be taken care of after the brain scan is complete."

Invincible.

The cotton of the gauze stings as it meets the open flesh, but I block it out of my mind, telling myself it was merely one of Buttons' cat toys instead of the point of a nail. Another nurse retrieves a wheelchair for me to sit in in order to avoid putting pressure on my foot, and I am wheeled down the dim hallways once more into a room.

The room is tight, no larger than the living room in my house. The walls are a sleek white, but are certainly not normal walls. They shine, and in their glimmer I catch a glance of my reflection. The look on my face startles me. I appear deranged.

The floor is lined with tiles as sleek as the walls, the crosses of the tiles suddenly stopping at the obstacle of a large glass pane. Behind the glass pane is a bulky machine, with a type of halo construction above a lone chair. A chair that will soon be occupied by me.

My thoughts come to a halt when the president towers over my wheelchair. He sticks out his hand, and I reluctantly shake it. "Pleasure to meet you, Platinum Woods." His smile is anything but genuine. "I'm going to give you a quick pep talk on how this procedure is going to go. Our hope is to run a smooth operation, as well as give you the most comfortable experience possible."

I nod. "Thank you, Mr. President."

"We're going to take you into a dark room. It might seem scary at first, but don't worry. Our very experienced doctors are going to hook up a lot of needles and wires to you, primarily in your head. To make sure we get the best results possible, you must sit completely still for ten minutes. A machine will swerve around your head, making a loud buzzing sound. It's fascinating, really. It collects your brain activity, takes x-rays, all that good stuff. After that, I will walk in and alert you when we've got what we need, and you are free to go. Have I made myself clear?"

I need to figure out a way to stall. "What exactly is the purpose of the different wires and needles?"

A cloud of stress seems to wash over the president's face. "The wires are in support of the machine, and the needles will be collecting blood and DNA samples. Do you have any other concerns, or may we proceed?"

Dammit. "You may proceed. Thank you."

He motions to the guards. "Wheel her into the lab."

In hardly any time at all, I am trapped behind the glass pane, similar to that of an animal caged in a pet shop. I've always felt bad for those animals; they seem to appear so frightened. I'm not frightened right now, though. Frightened is the feeling you get when you close your eyes and see blood and death. Right now, I'm vulnerable, the kind of vulnerable like someone has ripped all your clothes off and lights are shining on all of your scars; the ones on the outside and on the inside.

It takes the doctors longer than I thought, probably 30 minutes, to get everything in place. Then the lights flicker off, and they vanish into the dark.

In the darkness, I imagine I am no longer here, but instead playing hide and seek with my parents. I always hid behind the same chair in the dining room, and they'd pretend not to know where I am. Then my dad would come up behind me, pick me up by my waist, and spin me around in never-ending circles.

The dining room quickly fades from my imagination. A man enters through the door of one of the glass panes, and I squint to read his nametag: R. Layenne.

"Good morning Platinum. I'm Roger Layenne, and I'm in charge of your test today. Does everything feel okay? Any pain, numbing, uneasiness of any sort?"

I shake my head. "I'm fine, thank you."

"Good, good." He makes some marks on a clipboard, and I continue to answer a series of related questions for several minutes. When he's finally finished, he gazes up at me from his clipboard.

"Miss Woods," he adjusts his glasses. "This machine has been perfected by some of the best scientists in the world. There's no way to cheat, lie, or hide any of the results we gather here today. Do you understand?"

There are times in your life when it is better to let instinct overrule logic. This is one of those times. A voice in my head is screaming at me to run, and I must obey it.

I yank the dozens of cords out from my skin. The doctor takes a step back, clearly stunned. Mustering all my strength, I force my hands to wrap around his throat and push his body against the wall.

"Do not underestimate me, asshole. I can be a bitch when I want to be." Using my last bit of muscle, I throw his body through the glass.

Once I break through, time freezes. The guards raise their guns. The nurses rush to Doctor Layenne's aid.

And I run faster than I ever have in my life.

I make my way down to the infirmary, figuring I can temporarily hide there. Bullets chase after me, fortunately none of them hitting me; but I do hear a screech from one of the nurses. "He's dead, Roger's dead!" My heart pangs in my chest.

He can't be dead.

I don't have time to focus on that, though. When I arrive in the infirmary, the puncture on my foot has reopened, disabling the function of my leg. A pair of crutches with half the paint peeled off sit solitary by the door, as if waiting to be used. I grab them quickly, but then realize I hear footsteps. The guards are coming.

There's no possible way for me to escape without being shot. It dawns on me that the only thing I can do is surrender.

I fall to my knees, all hope lost, but two strong hands wrap around my waist, and I am pulled into a hidden room right before the guards spot me.

Once I'm inside, I spin around accusingly. "What the—"

"Shhh! They'll hear us." A young man with dark hair, tanned skin, and emerald eyes meets my gaze. He has some kind of magnetic aura about him, and I am intrigued.

I focus on my surroundings. We're in some sort of medication storage room. Shelves line the walls, littered with assorted pill bottles and liquid containers.

Once we hear the guards leave, words leap out of my mouth. "What just happened? Who are you? Where are we? Why did you just do that?"

He raises his hands defensively. "Geez, calm down."

I glare at him, exhaustion and pure insanity encompassing my brain. "You better explain, and you better explain now."

He sighs as if he's regretting what he's just done, and leans back against the shelves in a casual manner. How can he possibly be relaxed in a situation like this? "Nice to meet you too, Blondie. I'm Wren, a nurse-in-training. I've seen you around here before, and I like you. You're not like the other clueless and obedient patients. You seem to actually have a mind of your own." A teasing smile spreads upon his face, and I glance down, embarrassed.

"When I saw you crouched down, ready to give in to the guards, I couldn't let it happen. You deserve to get out of here. So I pulled you in here before you were caught. You're welcome, by the way." Wren winks.

"Thank you." I shift uncomfortably, glancing around awkwardly, but he keeps staring at me with those sparkly green eyes.

"So, what about you? You gotta name, or should I just call you Blondie?"

I shrug. "Whatever you prefer," I think he takes the comment flirtatiously, because the next thing out of his mouth completely stuns me. "You're way too pretty to be caged up in here."

Pretty? No one's ever called me pretty before.

"I'm not pretty," I start to say, but Wren interrupts.

"Are you kidding me? Blondie, you're practically a model."

I ignore his measly attempts at hitting on me. "Can I go now? I ran from the guards so I could escape this place, not so some random guy could flirt with me in a medicine closet."

The comment only makes him grin wider. "I knew you were feisty. Alright, but I would suggest getting that wound patched up first." He gestures to my foot.

I start to shake my head, but he hoists me up, cradling me in his arms. I don't feel like fighting back. He then gently lays me on a table and injects a needle in my vein.

Once I awaken, I notice he is already deep into stitching up the wound. My body stays motionless as he continues to sew the skin back together.

"I'll be sad when you leave," Wren whispers, but his focus still concentrated on my foot.

"Why?" I whisper back.

"Because," he murmurs, "I really like you."

Chills crawl up my spine. "But…but you don't even know me."

He glances up at me for a split second. "Of course I do."

I raise my eyebrows. "Prove it."

"Okay," he nods and clears his throat. "I know your name is Platinum, even though I'd much rather call you Blondie. You're sixteen years old, and you were sent here almost two weeks ago because you have dangerous unidentified brain capabilities."

My eyes widen, and he snickers at my reaction. "I'm a nurse. I keep track of everyone's files."

Oh. That makes sense.

A wave of silence closes in on us, and not another word is spoken until Wren's finished with the last stitch. "There. It's all good. I'd recommend not putting too much weight on that foot, though, or it could really cause you some pain." He stares at me affectionately.

"Stop it!" I scowl at him.

"Stop what?"

"Quit acting all flirty around me. It's weird and creepy. It's also extremely inconsiderate with the situation I'm in."

"What? A guy can't develop a crush on a cute girl? I'm sorry for being such a rebel."

"I am not afraid to hurt you, Wren."

"I believe you, Blondie. I saw what you did to that guy out there. It's pretty nasty." His eyes shimmer with amusement. Suddenly, his computer starts to beep, and a glowing red light flashes from the screen. Wren rushes towards it and presses several buttons that brings up a live newsfeed.

It's a reporter. She's standing right outside this building. "A sixteen-year-old girl by the name of Platinum Woods has claimed to have the ability to see the future of our nation. She is currently being held captive in this building right behind me."

This can't be happening.

The reporter continues. "Two days ago, Sixteen-year-old Platinum Woods opened these exit doors to escape the Government Mental Institution, but was later caught and brought back to her cell. Let's roll the footage of exactly what happened."

Suddenly, there I am on Wren's computer screen, the action shot just two days ago. It's unnerving to view myself as the rest of the nation must be viewing me. I look possessed. My skin is a grey-white color, as if all the blood had left my body. My blue eyes are crazed, peeled wide open, and my mouth gaping in shock. With my hospital gown, I look like those people you see in psychotic films, the patients who are screaming nonsense and on the verge of losing their minds.

The footage cuts off; the camera is focused back on the reporter. "The president has been avoiding the public eye, and has been spotted visiting the Government Mental Institution daily. People have gone into panic mode since Platinum appeared on camera, warning viewers about the future of America as we know it. Is the president plotting something? Is Platinum assisting him? We'll continue to follow this story and keep you updated. I'm Jessica Diamond, reporting for 31 Action News."

Slowly, Wren closes the lid to his laptop. He turns around to face me, totally expressionless.

"Wren," I cautiously step away from him, tears clouding my eyes. "Please don't hurt me. Please."

His hands slide through his hair, and he looks as if he's struggling internally. "I'm not going to hurt you, Blondie. I'd never do that. Not with a pretty face like yours."

My heart beat slows. "What happens now?"

His brows furrow. "Well, if I'm caught hiding you in here, it's like pointing a gun at my own head."

I start to worry. "Are you going to make me leave?"

He shakes his head, and looks at me as if I'm crazy. "No way. I'm not feeding you to the wolves."

I let my body sink to the floor and then gaze up at him hesitantly. "Thank you. I know you're taking a risk here, and I appreciate it."

He sits down across from me. "It's my second day working here, I might as well make an impression." He laughs, but his remark makes me feel worse than I already do.

"Why can't I just be normal, Wren?" I exhale a long overdue sigh of frustration. "How did I end up hiding in a medicine closet with a guy at some insane asylum?"

"It's because you're broken."

I'm slightly taken aback at his response. "What do you mean I'm broken?"

"You're broken in the eyes of society, so they put you in here to try and repair you."

I roll my eyes. "That's the most tragic and pathetic thing I've ever heard."

"It's not." He reaches out for my hand, and I dubiously let him hold it. "Blondie, have you ever seen a piece of glass shatter?"

"No. What does glass have to do with this conversation?"

"Let me finish. When the sun hits the glass just right, you can see the light shine through its cracks. It's not tragic. It's beautiful."

I want to ask him what cliché romance novel he stole that line from, but I keep my mouth shut. Maybe, just maybe, this guy does have some depth to him.

"Don't let them change you, okay? Promise me that one thing."

I look into his eyes and nod. "I promise."

***

A gunshot bursts the bubble of naivety surrounding me.

Guards enclose Wren and I in a tightknit circle. Fear washes over his face, but I try to mask any doubt I possess. I do not want to come off as weak.

"Young man." The president approaches us, his eyes sharper than daggers. "You should be expecting severe consequences for hiding a patient."

"As for you, Platinum." He looks like he's about to explode with anger. "Not only have you attempted escaping the government, but now you have killed one of the best neurosurgeons in the country."

My gut twists.

I am a murderer.

My face contorts with grief. "I killed Doctor Layenne?"

"Roger Layenne was found dead in the lab."

"I couldn't have killed him. There has to be some sort of mistake, Mr. President."

"No, there is no mistake. After you threw him through the glass, his head hit the sharp corner of a table. The impact to his head is what killed him."

I wretch, the graphic details burning into my mind, the thought too disgusting to picture.

The president shakes his head miserably. "I'm going to have to charge you with murder."

I try to plead with him, going far enough to use his own argument. "But sir, I'm not mentally stable. I don't have control over my actions."

The president continues to glare at me. "It'll be up to the criminal justice system to decide whether or not you'll be charged with murder."

Wren wraps his arm around me, and I lean into him, grateful for his presence.

"Hands off the girl." Wren quickly lifts his arm from my shoulder, and I shiver at the mere sound of the president's voice. He meets my eyes. "For now, Platinum, you're going to back to your cell. Wren, we'll set up a cell for you as well."

I feel the familiar steel of the handcuffs clasp around my wrists, a gun held forcefully to my back, and I am led away from the scene. I hear Wren cry out as the guards handcuff him and take him away. "Platinum!" He shrieks. Tears slip from eyes. I hear him holler my name again and again, until it's just a faint whisper. Then, nothing at all but the same, cold sound of silence.

That night, I crouch into a ball on my cot and stare at the cell door, my mind swept away in thought. So much has happened in these last two weeks, it's difficult to comprehend it all.

Every time I try to think of something else, my mind always drifts back to him. There's such a longing in my heart, I don't even know what to do. Should I smile, remembering our short time together this afternoon? Or should I cry, about being torn away from him? It's all too surreal.

I also think about Doctor Layenne. If I am charged with murder, I will never be able to leave this cell, which makes me nauseous just thinking about it.

I should go to sleep. Maybe I'll regain some of my sanity.

Right before my eyes shut, though, something strikes my attention.

An eerily familiar ponytail is attached to the head of one of one of the doctors standing outside of my cell. She's about 5'2, with smooth, tan skin. She shares my same stick-thin bone structure, though, and her hair is similar to mine, too; long, thin, and white-blonde. Platinum-like, almost.

Mom.

It has to be her.

I want to call out to her, but somehow my words aren't processing.

A figure approaches her, who is unmistakably my father. Though my eyes form tiny slits, I can trace his features accurately: his scruffy stubble, bright blue eyes, and the same white-blonde hair as my mother's. His hand rests on her shoulder, and they appear to be in deep conversation. Maybe this is like a scene from a movie, where the mother and father sneak in, pretending to be doctors, but in reality they're here to find their imprisoned daughter.

It's the only logical explanation I can ponder.

And here comes the president.

He marches up to my parents and launches into conversation with them. So many questions are running through my head. Do Emerald and Crimson know that Mom and Dad are here? Are they safe?

I shake my head, too dizzied by all of it, and struggle to eavesdrop on their conversation.

"What about the kids?" the president asks while looking at my parents expectantly.

My father steps forward. "Emerald and Crimson are tied up, their mouths taped. They shouldn't be able to escape; the rope we used was pretty strong."

The president nods. "Very well. They have any idea what's happening?"

"No, sir."

"Good, good."

My mother clears her throat. "How much longer until the plan comes into action, sir? Haven't we done enough sneaking around? Are all the injections prepared? I say we execute it as soon as possible."

The president shakes his head vigorously. "No, we are certainly not prepared. First off, we need to find a way to inject the medicine into the kids without it seeming suspicious. The kids themselves will be most difficult to fool. With all the intelligence they have stored up in their brains, they probably have a basic idea of what's going on, and are going to try to resist it as much as possible. Most likely, they don't know the medicine is Glocylic, but they probably know the injections have something to do with why they're being contained."

My mind starts to work. *Glocylic.* I've heard that word in science class before. I just need to remember what it means.

My mother shudders. "Are you sure injecting Glocylic in patients will be acceptable to citizens of America? There are going to be many questions about why so many people died while in quarantine, and you can't just tell reporters you poisoned 5,000 patients. You'll have to tell them why you did it, and that is obviously not an option."

Oh, right.

Poison.

Glocylic is a type of poison.

"Relax, Violet, I'll figure it out. Americans will believe anything. Nobody will suspect a thing. It will all work out in the end. My biggest worry right now is injecting the serum into all these kids before they leak their foolish information to the world about my actual intentions. Trust me. It's better that these kids are taken captive. They weren't meant to live in the real world. That's not how their DNA was built."

The look in the president's eye is none other than hunger and greed.

My parents nod, and the president walks away. Suddenly, the two of them spin around to face my cell, and I shut my eyes forcefully.

"Look, Red," my mother squeaks, "It's Platinum. Gosh, we haven't seen her in almost three weeks. You think she misses us?"

My father's voice turns to stone. "We've got to detach from these kids, Vi. They were never ours anyway."

My heart shatters.

Violet sighs. "I know. It felt like it though, sometimes. When we went on those picnics, and the kids would run around laughing, acting like they didn't have any cares in the world. It just warmed my heart. And they look so much like us, too! I know our only job was to watch their brain activity all these years, but I really felt like we made a connection with them."

"Stop the tears, Violet. We are not their actual parents. Our assignment was strictly science related. There's nothing in the contract that stated anything about growing emotional attachment. It's over now, so think of all the money we'll get! That's what warms my heart."

Through all the shock and anger coursing through my veins, the sadness is most overwhelming. My father – the man who tucked me into bed every night, the man who rode with me on rollercoasters and helped me with my homework – that man is gone.

I can hear my mother begin to cry. "You're telling me it actually pleasured you to tape Crimson's mouth shut? That it made you happy to tie Emerald's hands to that chair as she screamed at me to stop? It broke my heart most of all, though, to watch Platinum get taken away by those officers. Those kids were more than science experiments, Red, and if I had realized that before we signed the contract, I never would've agreed to do this."

"Violet," my father exhales. "This isn't part of our job. I'm sorry you 'made a connection' with those foolish children, but we have to go. We have to help the president. We need to leave those goddamn kids behind."

I can hear my mother whimper as my father drags her away. Tears slide down my cheeks. But then I hear footsteps dash towards my cell. My heart quickens.

"These are my kids, and nobody takes them away from me. I have had to do enough sneaking around for the last sixteen years. I've had to tell too many lies for a man who thinks it's right to genetically modify innocent children for his own use. I'm finished with it."

I hear a firm smack as my father slaps my mother. "Snap out of it, Violet! Our president is only doing what's best. Now come with me before you do something you regret."

"Oh, I won't regret this."

I've had enough silence.

"Mom!"

I scream at the top of my lungs and arise from the cot. My mother's smile is a sight for sore eyes. "Platinum! I'll get you out of there sweetie, don't you worry!"

I leap off my cot and race to the cell door, beginning to pound on it. My mother digs a key into the lock and is about to twist it, when I spot my father pointing a gun to the back of my mother's head.

"MOM!" I screech, and thank God my mother ducks down. But the bullet is fired, and comes right for my forehead. I get down just in time.

"Dad," I glare at him through the cell bars. "I'm sorry you think I'm a defect, because," I reach through the bars and grab the gun out his hands, "I'm probably smarter than you."

My father stares at his hands, stunned, then gazes softly at me. "Platinum! I didn't mean to fire at you, love bug. Now, give Daddy back his gun, okay?"

"Fuck you." I fire at his foot, and he yelps in pain, swearing as he grabs his foot. "What the hell was that for?" he grunts.

"That's for lying to me for sixteen years."

My father's face twists with rage. "The president's just trying to perfect our society, Platinum. It's better this way."

I drop the gun. "It's *better* this way?" I struggle to keep my tears from letting loose as I stare into the eyes of the ruthless stranger my father has become. "Okay, asshole. Tell me what's better. Tell me how great it is to control the lives of 5,000 people. Do you realize how sickening it is to hold people hostage and treat them as if they're nothing more than a piece of property? You're using us to your own advantage so you can just sit back and watch while the people being contained here are used as pawns to whatever little game it is the government is playing. You want to know what that's called, Red? It's called being afraid. You don't know how to deal with your problems, so you think you can magically—*poof!*—use other people to make them disappear from existence." I stamp my foot, its sound echoing throughout the metallic room. "If you think you can fool yourself by thinking you're perfecting society, then you are dead wrong. You're a horrible person who manipulates others into becoming your personal slaves. And if you think you can fool 5,000 kids like me into your little trap, then you are over estimating your power. Even if you somehow do manage to pull off this scheme of yours, well," I look right into his eyes. "You're just hurting yourself."

My father has veins popping out of his head. He sputters, as if what I just said confuses him. "I'm not hurting myself!"

"Oh yes you are. Tell me, Red. What is the president actually doing with all these kids?"

"They're defects. He's erasing all of the defects."

"Wrong!" I sigh, satisfied with my knowledge. "But let me warn you— after all, I can see the future." I smirk. "You may think he's your partner in crime, always at your side through thick and thin; but he is dangerously manipulative, Red. He is a tyrant. So watch your back."

As he turns around, I pick up the gun and shoot him.

***

My mother and I hobble away to a hidden corner of the asylum.

"My baby!" The two of us sink to the ground in exhaustion, and my mother showers me with kisses. "I'm so sorry that happened. You're probably wondering why I'm here, right?" She smiles sheepishly at me. She's so pretty, even after all that just happened. Wisps of pale blonde hair have come undone from her smooth ponytail, framing her tan face. Her eyes, light blue like mine, squint innocently, and her perfect cupid's bow lips reveal pearly white teeth.

I wrap my arms around her and bury my face into her shoulder. "I know everything."

She frowns guiltily and tries to wriggle from my grip, but I hold on. "Thank you."

We sit like that for what seems like hours, arms wrapped around each other, one dependent on the other. That's how it is in our mother-daughter relationship. I can't live without her, she can't live without me.

She pulls away and looks at me, tears forming in her eyes. "I just want you to know," she chokes up. "I love you. I always have, and I always will. I know it may not seem like it, since I've been lying to you for the past sixteen years. But Platinum, you are my daughter. I've raised you as my daughter, loved you as my daughter. It was never pretend, Platinum. I love you. And I hope you can forgive me, because I am so, so sorry. You and Emerald and Crimson are my children, and when it came time to decide between you guys or my job, it was obvious where my heart was."

I start to cry, and so does my mother. "Red always saw it as a job. He was always writing down every little thing you did, recording and sending video footage to the president. I thought he was crazy. You guys aren't subjects for a science project. You are children, who deserve loving parents. I wish I'd realized it sooner." She gives me a watery smile, and I hug her once more.

"I forgive you."

36

She kisses me on the head. "Thank you. That means a lot." All of a sudden, the color drains from her face. Her blue eyes widen. "Emerald and Crimson! Platinum, we have to get to them before your father does. We need to go. Now."

We race towards the exit, only to find guards blocking the door. "Where do you think you're going?" One of the guards glares at me.

My mother clamps her hand over my mouth. "Good day, guards. I saw this captive running loose, and now it seems I've caught her."

The guards nod approvingly. "Would you like us to help you get her back into her cell, Nurse Violet?"

My mother shakes her head. "No. The president has ordered me to take her outside. We're testing some new drugs and can't have any wandering eyes spotting the lab tests."

The guards raise their eyebrows "Isn't this the one who killed Doctor Layenne?"

My mother gulps. "Yes,"

"Be careful with her."

My mother nods, and we slip past the exit.

Wind engulfs me from head to toe, and the moon glitters like a spotlight. I reach up and touch the trees, the moment so wonderful and inexplicable. I am free. Yes, the worst is yet to come. But I am free.

And that's when the bullets start.

My mother and I sprint toward the building. I trail behind her and the stitches on my foot ache as my feet pound on the cement.

I go down, falling on the cement, my foot oozing blood. My mother doesn't deny her loyalty, though. She hoists me up, and keeps running towards the building, cradling me in her arms.

Bullets continue to fly past us. It's so dark; it's getting difficult to see.

Finally, we reach the wall of the asylum.

Violet turns to me. "If we can get onto the roof, we can likely shimmy down the other side on a drain pipe and escape." I trust that she knows where to go. However, there's nothing to grasp onto save towering bricks. Luckily, I spot a service ladder attached to a wall leading all the way up to the roof of the building. There's no way I can climb up with my badly injured foot.

Suddenly, my mother is handing me her tennis shoes. "Put these on." She starts her way up the ladder, her bare feet grasping the rings easily. I stand in shock. "Hurry, Platinum!" she screams. I slip on the shoes, and follow her, depending more on my arms than my feet.

The roof is so far away, and energy is bleeding from my body by the second. The guards are going to catch up with me eventually, or one of their bullets will hit me. I snake up the ladder, mustering all the strength I can. My mother is almost to the roof. If she can do it, so can I.

"C'mon, Platinum!" She hollers, and then disappears from sight. She's made it. She is safely on the roof.

My heart thunders against my chest. I can't fail her now. If I do, she'll have risked her life for nothing.

Then, I spot my mom. She's making her way down the ladder, her finger tips coming more and more within reach. I reach out, waiting to grab her hand, waiting for her to pull me up. Invincible. Invincible. Invincible.

I look out, and see the president glaring at me with his devious brown eyes. The guards have what seems like millions of guns targeted right at us, but apparently not able to get a good aim. My father is pleading to the president, who is shunning him. Reporters crowd the area, thousands of cameras directed at me as well. This is all because of me.

Then all oxygen is sucked from my lungs.

My mother's body is on the cement.

Lifeless.

For a minute, my mind is blank. I never saw her body fall, let alone even hit the ground. My eyes narrow, and I examine her body, watching blood blossom from her ribcage.

I feel like falling too.

But I see it. Her arm twitches, then her leg.

"Mom!" I screech as loud as my lungs can, hoping if she survived she'll have a chance of hearing me. "Don't give up!" Tears slip out from my eyes, and for a moment the constant pangs of gunfire are muted and the world is quiet.

When I open my eyes, I have to rub them again to make sure my vision isn't hazy. My mother is climbing back up the pole. She's tied her shirt around her ribcage to stop the bleeding, and has resorted to wearing just a bra and jeans. I don't care, though. She's alive, and she didn't give up on me.

My heart bursts. We're going to make it. We're going to make it. The two of us, exhausted, bleeding, are going to make it out of this insanity alive.

"Platinum!" A man calls from the mass of people.

Wren.

I gaze out into the crowd until I meet his sparkly green eyes. Guards are struggling to restrain him as he fights against their grasp, but he manages to smile. He blows me a kiss, and I grin from ear to ear in spite of the situation.

"Honey," my mother rasps. She takes my hand, hers cold and clammy, mine radiating warmth. We inch up the pole together, defying all odds, determination in our eyes.

Truly, I do not comprehend it at all. I do not understand how my mom is climbing a building with a bullet in her rib cage. I do not understand how I am doing it myself. I do not understand the president, or my father, or whatever they're trying to plan. In fact, I don't understand anything.

But maybe it's okay to not understand. Maybe it's okay not to understand everything in this screwed-up world. Maybe the things you don't understand are the things that keep you going in life. The things that help you see the beauty, the chaos, and everything in between.

My thoughts are twisted when something sharp strikes my head. My vision goes blurry. So much pain.

I fall down, down, down. The last thing I see is my mother, screaming, reaching her hand out towards me.

I hit the cement.

Everything goes black.

Part 2

Ever

"Stop." My green eyes glare at my parents as they stumble through the entry hall, their words slurring together. My mother leans against the wall for stability, and my father wobbles, as if the wooden floor had turned to ice. Their eyes are bloodshot, clothes tattered, and the stench of beer and vodka wafts around them. A pair of homeless people.

"God, get it together!" I slam the front door of the house they had carelessly left open on their way in, and struggle to keep my tears from escaping. My hands anxiously tug on my fiery red ponytail. They have crossed the line this time.

"Do you know what time it is?" My voice wavers. "It's 3:00 a.m.!" Tears begin to slide down my cheeks. It's too much. "You left the house *twelve hours* ago! You told me you were going to the freakin' grocery store!" I curse under my breath as I walk up to my father. I slap him, hard. "I hate you. I hate you so much."

My mother sets her hand on my shoulder, but I smack it away. "I hate you too. If I could, I would move in with Wren!"

"Sweetie," my mother rubs her eyes in frustration. "Can we discuss this later?"

I slap her, too, harder than my father. "No. I am your child. You are supposed to take care of me. Sorry, but I don't consider running off to get high as positive parental guidance."

My parents stumble over to the living room and collapse on the sofa. This ends now.

"I am sick of being the adult around here! You need to get your shitty lives together! I can't sit here day after day, staring out the window, wondering 'Are they okay? When will they come home? Will they ever come home?' It *worries* me. But at least I'm not drinking a bottle of wine like half the other kids in West Lake to push my worries aside. You need to stop. I hate labeling my parents as drug addicts, but that is what you are."

I inhale a gulp of air, and my parents stare blankly at me. My words had absolutely no effect, of course.

"I'm calling Wren."

And I do, thinking my words over as I hear the click of each button. I press the cellphone to my ear, and shove stray stands of red hair away from my face.

"Ever?" my name echoes from his voice, as he answers my call on the first ring.

I breathe a sigh of relief. "Hi," I squeak. "Can you come pick me up?"

He hesitates for a moment, but his response is firm. "Sure."

"Thanks,"

I hang up, and listen to the resigning sound of the dial tone for a moment. Finally, I swivel around to face my parents. "I'm leaving."

My father rises from the sofa, livid. "You're not going anywhere!"

I nod slowly. "Yes, I am."

"Bullshit! You're not going off with that boy in the middle of the night! You're a sixteen-year-old girl who has no mind of her own!"

"That boy has a name." My tan skin flushes. "If you're allowed to go and get high in the middle of the night, then I'm allowed to do this! Wren cares about my existence, and I want to be with people who actually care that I'm alive! Don't pretend that you do. I know you wish I was dead. You've told me *to my face* that you wish I was never even born."

My father crosses his arms. "I was drunk, Ever. I didn't mean those things. You are staying here, and that is final."

The house gets strangely silent, like the quiet before the storm.

"I am leaving. For good."

He stalks towards me, his face twisted in anger. My father's hands reach out, and he lunges for my neck. I duck away in time.

"You sick murderer!" I scream at the top of my lungs. "You asshole! You absolutely psychotic asshole!"

He flings open the kitchen cupboards and grabs as many glass dishes as he can, launching them towards me at the speed of light. I dodge every one, until a glass hits my face. It shatters. I screech in pain as glass slices my skin, and I shut my eyes, careful to make sure none of it slips through my eyelids.

More glass breaks; but this time, it's the front door. I cautiously open my emerald eyes, and I spot Wren racing towards my father. Glass is lodged in his knuckles. He punched through the door. Wren wraps his hands around my father's neck, not strong enough to kill him, but enough to strain his lungs, for sure.

"Do it, Ever!" Wren calls to me, desperately. "You know what to do!"

My father's head turns towards me, his face a pale shade of blue. My mother curls in a ball on the sofa, her eyes wide with fear.

I'm scared.

He's my father.

But he tried to kill you, the little voices in my head whisper. *He tried to kill you.*

I nod, and stare straight into his eyes, careful not to distract my focus; I can only conjure the power on rare occasions.

The seconds eerily count down.

Ten…nine…eight…

Five…four…three…

Last chance.

Two…One…

I blink. It happens. My father's skin transforms to a ghostly pale, and his caramel eyes are soon the color of storm clouds. He howls in pain.

"What have you done, Ever?" His muscles contract in odd spasms and his body contorts in a way I never thought was humanly possible. His skin hardens.

I stumble back, my heart dramatically racing. This was the right thing to do.

"I will haunt you," my father utters his last words before he turns to stone.

———

Seconds later, I am surrounded by the comfort and safety of Wren's car. Leaning against the window, I heave, my breaths slow and shaky. I untie my hair from its ponytail and finger through its long red strands. My eyes instantly cloud with tears.

Wren leaps into the driver's seat beside me and pulls me to him. I feel secure with his tan, muscular arms wrapped around my small, frail body. We sit like that for what seems like ages.

Finally, he pulls away from me, and his green eyes meet mine.

"Ever," he whispers faintly, "I am so proud of you."

I can't hold the tears in any longer. They creep down my cheeks, slow and painful.

"I killed him." I murmur. "Am I just as guilty as him? Do I deserve to die too?" Sobs shake my body uncontrollably.

"Of course not!" Wren strokes my hair. "You just turned him to stone."

"Yeah, Wren. I just turned my own father to stone, no biggy."

"I didn't mean it like that."

I pull him in for a kiss, momentarily shutting him up. "I know."

Wren grins amusingly.

Playfully, I punch his bicep, momentarily forgetting my tears. Wren kisses my forehead. "I know that was scary. But it's over now. Control your powers."

I lean back against the seat and shut my eyes, exhausted and bewildered. And I see a girl.

She's not what you'd call vanilla pretty, but more like rocky road pretty. She's a little more unique-looking, with wavy platinum-colored hair and snow white skin, with pale blue eyes.

She is falling from a building, her head covered in blood.

I try to awaken, but I can't. An unknown force has sewn my eyes shut, and all I can see is blood slowly crawling through the girl's hair, inch by inch.

"Ever!" Wren's voice seeps into my brain, and my eyes burst open.

Wren stares at me, looking overly concerned. "You were screaming. Is everything alright?"

Something urges me to tell him the truth, tugging on my heart. Recently, every time I shut my eyes I see a blonde girl getting shot. Dead bodies are littering the streets. And every time I stare at something for more than ten seconds, there is a possibility that my conscience could lose control and the victim could turn to stone.

That's what I want to say.

But I don't. Nobody would understand, not even Wren.

I grin unconvincingly. "Peachy. Let's get out of here."

And we do.

We drive around town all night long, silence filling the gap between us. I open the car window and gaze at the stars, wondering what it's like to be normal. Or at least pretend to be normal. To feel normal.

Wren finally pulls up into the driveway of his house. His car clock blinks brightly at us: 6:02am.

"You're never going back to your house, are you? To your mom?"

Vigorously, I shake my head. "Never."

Wren sighs nervously. "I'm starting my new job tomorrow."

My hearts stops, just for a minute. Without Wren, I didn't have anywhere to go.

"But I'll be home at six. You can stay at my place. I won't mind. I'm going to train to be a nurse at the Government Mental Institution."

My body shudders. Rumors have been floating around town recently, and I've heard some dangerous captive is being held there and the government is having a panic attack.

I lean towards Wren and press my lips to his. "Be careful," Two words, but two very important ones.

***

I awaken in a bed that is not my own. It feels surreal.

I'm hallucinating, wandering around Wren's bedroom, colors dancing before my eyes; the aftermath of using my powers. A migraine begins to build in my head, pressurizing my brain, and random words shoot out of my lips. I'm on the brink of death. Energy is slowly seeping from my veins.

Stepping into the bathroom and facing the mirror, I stare into the eyes of a girl who is not me.

Instead of a sixteen-year-old woman, the girl is a mere twelve-year-old child. She has long red hair that seems to have lost its vibrant shade, and her tan skin is almost sickly-looking. Her eyes not a bright green, but a watery grey, with dark circles formed under them. Scars weave across her once pure smooth skin, like she is a broken porcelain doll that was glued back together.

She is not me. She is not Ever.

But that's what I feel like. I feel as if my parents have shattered me into pieces, and I tried to pick up the remains of my soul and put it back together, but I am unfixable. I have too many scars on the outside, and even more on the inside. Never will I be truly healed.

A solemn sigh escapes my lips. I hobble down the stairs of Wren's home, where his mother greets me.

"Hello, Ever," she hugs me and kisses my head affectionately. "How are you, dear?"

I nod and give Ivory a small smile, and she returns it with sympathy swimming in her eyes.

It is obvious that Wren got his attractive looks from his mother, both of them possessing the same curly black hair, big green eyes, and olive skin, with a grin that can light up a room more than any star.

"Wren told me you had a bit of family trouble, and that you'd be staying with us for a little while. Is that right?" Her voice is like a lullaby, and it makes me want to fall asleep to its soothing sound.

"Yes, I had an unfortunate fallout with my parents last night." My cheeks flush, embarrassed. Ivory bites her lip. She knows about my parents' issues. I don't mind, though. She acts more like my parent than my mother and father ever were. I tell her about my troubles, and she always has nourishing advice.

"May I walk outside and get some fresh air?"

"Of course," Ivory unlocks the front door and I step out into the serenity of a rainy winter afternoon.

I circle the neighborhood countless times, just me and my thoughts, and a strange feeling begins to course through my veins; freedom. My mother and father were a constant pressure, weighing me down with fear whenever they wouldn't return. Now, I am free of their burden.

As I wander around a cul-de-sac, I spot a forest behind one of the houses. My curiosity gets the best of me, and I trample through the foliage. Brittle leaves weave above me, shading the pattering rain drops and brewing storm clouds as I follow a dusted wooden trail. I am lost in daydreams of a perfect world, a world without the abuse of my parents, without the days where I sat alone at the playground, day after day, friendless and alone. My life had no purpose until I saw Wren that fateful day in the ninth grade wing.

Suddenly, I hear footsteps near me, stopping my feet dead in their tracks.

A man's voice comes over a walkie-talkie.

"Yes, we need you to scope her out."

"Roger that."

Shit.

I duck behind a tree just as the guy swivels around to look in my direction. He is armed with guns, tranquilizers, and knives, as if he is about to go hunt down some vicious animal.

"What's the physical description?" the man speaks into the walkie-talkie.

"Red hair, green eyes, tan skin. Thin, but not drastically skinny. About five-foot-two. The name is Stone."

"Where was she last seen?"

"Last recorded sighting was entering the home of Aspen and Ivory Smith. The home has one adolescent resident, Wren Smith."

"Copy that."

My heart starts to thud, and my foot moves a single inch, managing to rustle some leaves.

Before I can even blink, a gun is pressed to my head.

"If you move, I will shoot you."

Well, that was blunt. I don't move a muscle.

"I've got her captured!" The man shouts into the device. "I repeat, the captive is apprehended! My location is north fifty-three. Send out help, she's a dangerous one."

Dangerous one?

In one motion, I grab a knife from the man's tool belt and press it up against his throat, not afraid to slash his neck wide open. We stand there, both terrified, me at gunpoint and him in fear of his throat being slit.

"You may think you're strong," I whisper. "But I am stronger."

And I am.

How many other people have the power of turning their enemies to stone?

"If you let me go, you won't lose your life. You won't die today."

The man lets his guard down for a moment, a look of terror flashing in his dark brown eyes. Then he puts his shield back up, trying to pull his strength together, his eyes once again cold and hard.

"Yeah, Stone? You think you have a chance of killing me?"

My whole life plays before my eyes, like some disaster movie, every horrific moment.

I inhale a gulp of air, flames burning in my eyes. "You are going to regret those words. I will murder you, and I am determined to make it the most painful and intense experience you have ever lived through. Except, this time, you will not live. You will die."

The gun fires.

I successfully duck under the bullet, and it zooms right past my forehead, hitting a tree trunk instead. I brace myself, and stab the knife right into his thigh. He lets out a scream, one that pierces my ears as the guilt overwhelms me. The man falls to the ground, his body contorting on the forest floor. I wretch as the blood begins to pour from his leg, soaking into the nearby snow.

I almost feel guilty, but I remind myself— he tried to kill me.

I stare into his eyes, his wide and blank, mine narrow and focused. I force my mind to lose all train of thought, all control of my conscience.

The dreadful seconds begin to count down, and the process starts.

I watch his skin harden, bit by bit, and once it's finished, I collapse on the ground and sob. In two days, I've murdered two people. Not only that, but I used my vicious power against them. It is a curse. I am a curse. I am no better than my father, and his sick and greedy ways.

"Why?" I call out to the sky. "Why did you do this to me?"

Thunder strikes, and rain showers from the heavens. My tears run with it, slow and heavy, full of grief.

I hear the police sirens, echoing like a warning sign. *We're coming!* The government was saying. *We will get you, Ever Stone! And we will find out what you're hiding, every last bit of it.*

So, I run.

My sneakers become soaked as I sprint on the sludgy forest ground, away from the evil government, away from the struggles of reality. The jeans I'm currently wearing are drenched from the rain, and my white V-neck is splattered with dirt and contains absolutely no warmth in the freezing weather. I shove my wet red hair away from my face, and continue to sprint as if my life depends on it. Because it does.

As I run though, something makes me pause. Shadowy figures come into view. One of them is my father. The other is the man I just killed. Their spirits drift towards me. The police are racing at me from the other direction.

I have always been capable of handling things myself. I have always had a rough but stable enough path ahead of me. But I am at a dead end. There is, for the first time in my life, nowhere to run.

***

This place is familiar.

I have been here before, I know it.

But at the same time, I don't recognize it at all.

But the walls…

Suddenly, I know. The visions. They take me here, to this confined hospital. I know this place like the back of my hand. And the girl! The platinum-haired girl in my visions! She must be here too. I wonder if she knows what this is all about. I wonder if she knows why this is happening.

But how did I get here? The last thing I remember was attacking the police; then everything went black.

I glance at my surroundings. It's just a typical hospital room. Staring at my clothes, I notice someone, most likely a nurse, has bathed and clothed me in a fresh hospital gown. My hair is once again silky and vibrant, and as I grasp a hand-mirror from my bedside table, I see that my eyes are bright, skin smooth. I'm the picture of health.

My ears catch the sound of a nurse's footsteps approaching. Quickly, I shut my eyes and pretend to sleep.

"Sir, she's still asleep." A woman's voice squeaks.

A man comes up to stand next to her. I can tell by the sound of his shoes that he's male, and most likely a doctor. "That's the trick of the serum. It knocks you out for a full 72-hour period."

Seventy-two hours? I've been knocked out for a full 72 hours? My heart starts to race. I have to get out of here. Who knows what that serum does to my mind? I could end up confessing secrets that aren't meant to be spoken of.

"But, it's been almost four days, doctor." Worry drips through the nurse's tone, only confirming my fears.

"Perhaps Dreyden injected a little more than necessary,"

"When's the test?"

"Tomorrow at noon. Doctor Roger Layenne will be screening her, as neurology is his expertise." The doctor seems so content. It worries me.

The nurse shuffles through several papers. "Where's the patient schedule? I seem to have lost it."

"No problem, I have it memorized. Tomorrow is the scan for Patient 3072, Platinum Woods. The day after is the scan for Patient 3073, Ever Stone."

Platinum Woods; an alarm goes off in my head as soon as the name is said. A sense of familiarity comes over me, as if we have already met.

"Thank you. Will Miss Stone be moved into a cell anytime soon?"

The doctor clears his throat. "Not yet. Her mental condition is far too unstable. We need to have further examination of the patient before she is allowed into a cell."

Once the doctor leaves the room, I force my eyelids to crack open, absorbing the fluorescent lighting.

"Hello, Miss Stone. How are you feeling? I am Nurse Violet, and I will be at your aid during the time you spend here."

She looks into my eyes with a motherly gaze. Her looks are very similar to the girl in my visions. They both possess the same white-blonde hair, pale blue eyes, and slim bone structure.

"I am well, thank you Violet." I respond, even though my head feels like it is going to explode with pressure. "I do have a couple questions, though. Where am I, and why am I here?"

Violet's friendly eyes grow dark and weary. Her radiant cheeks turn stark, and her lips quiver with anxiety.

Why is she so nervous? What is she hiding?

"Those questions are currently unanswerable; the answers are protected by the government's national security."

You've got to be joking with me. I raise my eyebrows and glare at the poor nurse, who obviously isn't good at creating excuses. "Violet, as a person, I have rights to know where I am, and why I am in that location. Because right now, it looks like I've been kidnapped, or—"

The back of my neck starts to tingle. The tingling slowly spreads throughout my body, like it's sizzling my blood. My already agonizing migraine doubles. No, triples. I scream as loud as my lungs can manage. The only way the pain could be numbed is if someone shot me.

Violet seems confused, as if she wasn't expecting this reaction and has no idea how to stop it. "Dreyden!" she shrieks.

A guy races into the room. The pain drains from my neck for a split second, and I am trapped in his alluring looks that would make the heart of any woman melt.

A sandy-blonde shade colors his messy curls. Soulful brown eyes meet my green ones. There is thought behind them, and I can tell he is an intelligent man.

"What's wrong? Is someone dead?"

"I don't know!" Violet sobs. "I've never seen this reaction before in a patient!"

Dreyden rushes over towards me, and his hand reaches for the back of my neck. He pokes at it, and I wince at the sting of his touch.

"We need to check her blood. Get me a syringe and tourniquet, now."

Violet sprints out of the room, and Dreyden kneels next to me.

"Hey, it's going to be okay." His hand strokes my arm, and I shudder at the sensation. "What's your name?"

"Ever Stone." I whisper.

The color drains from Dreyden's face.

"What?" I squeak. "Why do you look so scared? What's wrong with me?"

"Violet!" He calls. "Get in here!"

Violet returns in a flash, holding a syringe and tourniquet. The next few minutes are pure silence. Dreyden sticks the needle in my skin, and I slowly watch him gather my blood in a tube.

"Nothing's wrong with you, Ever." He casts a sad look at me, his eyes filling with tears. "You just killed my brother."

I gasp. My hand flies to my mouth, and for a second, I can't breathe. "Was he the guy who tried to capture me before the police came?"

Dreyden nods. "Yes. His name was Foe. Foe's job is—was to pinpoint all the captives, which is very dangerous, as the captives can sometimes retaliate. But it's very rare, and if a captive does retaliate, it's usually not deathly." He stares into my eyes, as if he's searching for something. "So, I guess you're pretty special."

A wave of grief comes over my body. "I'm so sorry. Really, I am."

Dreyden's eyes glisten with tears. "I help the police locate captives if they need an extra set of hands. They just so happened to ask for my assistance today. When I found him dead at the site, I immediately asked who killed him. The other guys said it was the captive's doing. And that her name was Ever. Ever Stone." He looks intently at me. "So how'd you do it?"

My eyebrows furrow together. "How'd I do what?"

"How'd you murder him?"

I gulp. "Can I choose not to answer?"

His eyes narrow sharply. "Is it so wrong to wonder how you killed my sibling?"

My eyes narrow in response. "Is it so wrong to wonder what the hell I'm doing here?"

Dreyden looks back at Violet, whose eyes are filled with curiosity. "Violet, can you please excuse yourself from the room?"

She sulks, but the nurse exits the room without reprisal. Dreyden once again meets my gaze.

"Okay, look, it's kind of my job not to tell patients anything. Usually they never ask, though. But for some reason," his brow furrows, "the serum that was injected is having absolutely no effect on you."

"I'm gonna believe that's a good thing."

"Can I ask you a question?"

"Certainly."

Dreyden looks at me with a studious expression. "Why are you so different than all the other patients?"

I smirk cunningly. "Everyone has their secrets."

***

As Dreyden exits my room, I pull on the separation curtain. On the other side is a man, who appears to be enveloped in a coma. I read his name tag; Hawk. No last name. Just Hawk. He intrigues me, certainly.

Before my curiosity gets the best of me, Violet returns to my room.

"Is there anything you need, miss?"

"Yes. Some answers." I twirl my hair innocently around my finger. "For instance, tell me what hospital I'm at. I deserve to know that much."

She finally gives in. "You're currently staying at GMI Infirmary and Caretaking for the Psychologically Unstable."

It takes me a minute for the words to finally connect. "I'm at the Government Mental Institution!? So basically an insane asylum."

"Please don't question my answers, Miss Stone. Besides, you need some rest. I'll be right back with your snack. The cafeteria is serving Tapioca pudding today." She smiles and walks away, blonde ponytail swishing behind her.

Millions of thoughts begin rocketing through my mind. Does the government know about my powers? What are they going to do after my screening tomorrow? Does Wren know where I am? Does he know how much I miss him? Is he freaking out?

There are so many unanswered questions.

A feeling of nausea twists my stomach. There are currently no nurses supervising me, but I'm sure it won't matter if I go get some antacid from the infirmary.

The ragged slippers covering my feet slide across the sleek tile flooring. I stumble through hallways until I reach a sign with *Infirmary* scrawled on it with ink pen. My stomach squeezes together, as if it was pierced by a knife. I need to find that antacid.

I rummage through cabinet after cabinet, becoming wearier by each second. Finally, my eyes fall on a door that blends into the beige colored walls; the only place I haven't searched. I grasp the handle firmly and yank it open.

My heart stops.

Beat, beat… beat, beat… beat, beat… beat… beat… beat…

He is there. He is there with her.

I cannot move.

Not a sound is heard, except for the faint chatter of distant nurses. His green eyes meet mine, and I am hypnotized. I am trapped, but not afraid.

It's all in slow motion, really. He opens his mouth, yet all that comes out is jumbled syllables. My ears do not catch them. They reject them, leaving the words hanging in midair like a bunch of puppets drooping from their strings. His eyes, they crinkle at the corners. The tears still sneak through, however, snaking down his cheeks, outlining every crack in the skin. He grabs his drooping puppets, trying to make a show out of them, but I have no intent of watching. I already know who dies in the end. Me.

The girl. She lies in his arms, eyes shut, silent as a corpse. She's still breathing though. Her stomach rises and falls in rhythm.

I recognize her. She is the girl from my visions.

I spin around, my ponytail slapping his face. My brain forces my feet to move. Each step is a thud, shaking the floor. I am an earthquake, destroying everything in my path.

Goodbye, Wren.

When I reach the bathroom, I lean over the sink. My breaths come rapidly. I need to scream, and so I do, letting it echo through the room.

I let myself fall to the floor.

I've made sure that throughout this hell that is my life, I've always had an angel; Wren. He has been my savior, bringing me to Heaven when I was lured to the Underworld. No longer.

The demons arrive. Their names are Depression, Anger, and Loneliness.

Depression gives me a bucket of tears. He floods my eyes, making me sob and sob and sob until my eyes have hardened. All of the moisture has been sucked from my body. He slashes my heart open, leaving a crack that will never truly heal.

Anger steals my soul, blackening it with the darkest ash. He lights a flame inside of me, the flames engulfing me until my heart is burnt to its core. Eternal rage courses through my veins.

Loneliness; the worst of all. She is tiny yet strong. She hands me a cloak, which I obediently slip over my head, letting my red hair fall around it. But this isn't any normal cloak. It blocks out the rest of the world. It makes you feel like nobody in the universe cares for your existence. Nobody at all. She gives me a sad smile, and pulls a Sharpie from her pocket, scribbling words on my broken heart: worthless, unwanted, useless.

The demons finally leave. I call after them, but they don't look back. I want them here with me. Currently, they are my only friends.

Wren kissed her. I know for a fact that I didn't imagine it. He put his lips on hers, a slow kiss, and if she had been awake, she would've savored every second of it.

Now it's clear as day to me as to why he took this job; to hook up with girls. Girls who are possibly completely insane. Then again, am I an improvement from these girls? No, I am not. I was raised by addicts, and I possess powers of an unknown origin. When Wren and I first met, I could tell he was smitten with me. I'm not trying to sound conceited, but I'm a very attractive young woman; boys flirt with me all the time. Wren and I had an amazing relationship for about two months—until I finally confessed who I truly I am. That this "flawless" life I live is a lie. He supported me, of course. But over the couple years, my life at home became worse and worse, and we no longer had a normal relationship. We slowly stopped going out on dates. He was more of a hero, saving a damsel in distress over and over again. Wren would keep his phone on at night, making sure if I ever called he'd be there to rescue me. As much as I tried to deny it, our relationship had become solely centered around the danger between me and my parents. The feelings of love and passion that had once thrived between us were gone.

And he decided to take a break from it for a little while by cheating on me.

I wrote his name on my heart in permanent marker. He wrote mine on his in pencil.

Just like the rest of my life, my love for Wren slowly crumpled up in a tight little ball and was tossed down into the fiery depths of Hell, never to return.

***

I am swimming in a pool of brown eyes.

They are so beautiful, filled with sparkles of gold. I could float within them forever, right into his soul, so pure and gentle. His eyes are graced with wonders of such spirit; I cannot fathom their inevitable perfection.

"Ever?"

I am instantly pulled out of the pool, cold and shaking. For a moment, I was lost, and I didn't want to be found.

"Yes, Dreyden?"

"Are you okay?"

I wanted to scream. What a pathetic excuse for a question. How could I be anywhere near okay with all I've went through? The mere amounts of goodness I once had are now shattered with the rest of my life. I don't see a reason to live anymore.

"You do matter, Ever."

I shake my head, confused. "Did I say that out loud?"

His hand strokes my cheek. "Get some rest. I'll wake you up when dinner is prepared."

Dreyden exits my room, and all I can think about is how maybe someone does care about me after all.

I awaken to a powerful screech, ricocheting off of the walls. Quickly, I yank the separation curtains back, only to see that Hawk is convulsing. His muscles jerk with such force I have to lean away. The unsettling part, though, is his eyes, which are a gorgeous shade of dark violet but are peeled wide open; drops of blood are leaking from the corners. I heave a little in my mouth.

Dreyden leaps into the room, making eye contact with me. "What did you do to this patient!?"

Cowering in fear, I reply. "I didn't do anything! I was asleep until his machine went haywire, and I pulled back the curtains to find him like this!"

"What the hell?" he mutters, studying the patient, struggling to make sense of his current state. Dreyden yells into his walkie-talkie, "We have a situation! Patient 3074, Hawk Doe, is showing signs of unstable health. Report to the ER immediately!"

People rush into the room all at once. The doctors don't take action, though. It's as if they're completely baffled. I overhear snippets of conversation:

"He was in a coma, not expected to wake up…"

"We stopped treatment last week. He was supposed to die any day now…"

"This is impossible! I don't understand…"

As Dreyden continues to calm panicked nurses, something falls out of his pocket. A piece of paper. I reach down and pick it up. It's an envelope with a foreign postmark. The corners are yellowed, and the hand writing is barely legible. Something that makes the acid in my stomach rise, though, is a streak of red across the front flap of the envelope. It is eerily similar to that of human blood.

Without the attention of prying eyes, I open up the letter and take a quick peek. What I read astonishes me.

The words are extremely difficult to make out, but what I manage to read is about a group of tyrants, slowly taking control of the diverse governments of the nations with their bloodthirsty greed. Most of it is absolutely morbid, and a rush of fear pulses inside me. When I get to the part about how those born with unique powers must be used as weaponry, I start to question my own self. Am I one of them?

 "EMMALINE!"

On top of his mental breakdown, Hawk begins to scream *Emmaline* repeatedly; until I know for a fact the name is seared into my brain. I like the name. It means "peaceful home," something I've always wanted to have.

"Did his girlfriend cheat on him or something? Trust me, I know the pain." I say this jokingly, expecting at least some pity laughs, but I get none.

"What does it mean then? Who's Emmaline?"

A nurse turns towards me with wide eyes.

"Emmaline is the name of his dead sister."

———

As boredom begins to take over my mind, I decide I can no longer brush off the incident that occurred with Hawk earlier. Violet had left her laptop in my room earlier; I grab it and choose to do some research of my own.

Nobody knows Hawk's legal last name, so I enter *Hawk* in the search bar. Of course, what pulls up is a list of different types of hawks in West Lake. Go figure.

When I search the keywords *Hawk, Emmaline* I finally get some results. Lucky for me, Emmaline doesn't seem to be a popular name.

I click on article after article. What I learn is this:

Hendrix Asher (or as everyone called him, Hawk), sixteen, is the oldest of five siblings. The youngest sibling, Emmaline Asher, was killed in a house fire eleven months ago (age five at the time of her death). Hawk was the one who caused the fire.

Hawk's father abused him from an early age, around age five, and he never dared to tell a soul. Eventually, Hawk got fed up. It was time for his father to receive the pain he had endured for the last eleven years.

When Hawk assumed everyone was out of the house except for his father, he set a tiny clump of gun powder on the kitchen floor. After he sparked the fire, he dashed outside the house at lightning speed. Hawk knew the consequences, but he didn't care. He wanted his father gone.

The explosion was much too powerful. The firemen found a total of three bodies on the property. Hawk Asher, lying motionless in the front lawn, was found comatose. Demarcus Asher, his father, found dead at the site. And Emmaline Asher, also found dead at the site.

Tears start to crawl down my cheeks. How horrible! I can't begin to ponder the awful truth of child abuse, and how Hawk had to go to intense measures to make it stop. The emotional abuse I went through with my parents was awful enough, but I can't comprehend his physical abuse. He could never live with the guilt of killing his sister, though, I know that. I certainly couldn't.

But he hadn't woken from his coma yet. He doesn't know he killed his sister...

Or does he?

Eventually, I put the research to rest, leaving me to wonder about the mystery that is Hendrix Asher.

***

It is time for my therapy session. It is agonizing, but according to Violet "it helps us to see how you're doing psychologically.", or whatever that means. I walk into the therapist's office, but instead come face-to face with Dreyden.

"Why are you here?" My eyes graze his sharp jawline and mysterious eyes. His sandy curls are tussled, but not in a sexy way. More like, 'I'm really stressed so please do not screw around with me.'

"I'm filling in for your therapist."

"Don't you have to be, like, I don't know, an actual therapist to do that?"

"I'm really not in the mood for your shit today, Ever, so if you could sit down and shut up, it would be much appreciated."

Reluctantly, I sit down in the swivel chair, but my stone-hard gaze does not disappear.

"You do realize that you're not getting a single word out of me, right? If I were you, I wouldn't even bother trying."

He sits there for probably a full minute, staring at me, trying to mess with my head. "You would get along really well with one of my other patients. You're both sarcastic and stubborn."

"And who might that be?" I ask him teasingly.

"That might be Platinum Woods. You know her? She's a bit quiet, but she's not afraid to speak her mind when she feels like it."

I shake my head, but I feel the blush climbing up towards my cheeks. I cannot give away my visions. "No, I don't. I do, however, like her name. Very pleasant and fragile."

"I like your name better."

A laugh escapes my mouth; I can't help it. "Why? Who in their right mind names their daughter Ever? Oh, right, I forgot. My parents didn't have right minds. They were wrong minds all the way."

Dreyden smiles, his eyes crinkling at the corners. "I think they named you Ever because you were born to be a legacy."

His response puzzles me. "Anyway, back to therapy. Fire away with your questions."

"Alrighty," he flips through some files until he comes to what I guess is mine. "Do you have any idea why you're here, Miss Stone?"

I decide to play this off cool and casual. "Nope."

"Have you ever had any unexplainable experiences? For instance, unique powers, strange visions, the like."

"Nope."

"I have all of your files right here, Ever, from the day you were born. I know all about you. You can't lie through your teeth."

My shoulders go up in a shrug. "Well, there's nothing going through my teeth, because I'm not lying."

His hands run through his hair, messing it up even more. "So you're telling me that Foe was just hardened to stone by Mother Nature?"

 Well, I am officially screwed.

"No comment."

Dreyden leans towards me until our noses touch. I can smell the beer coming from his breath; most likely a stress reliever. I count the tiny freckles on his cheeks and nose, all seventeen of them.

"You were not coincidentally born with your powers, Ever. They're from something entirely different."

He stands up and walks away. I can't take the suspense.

"It's The Forces, isn't it?"

The look on his face says it all. "How the hell do you know about that?"

I grasp the letter from the pocket in my hospital gown and hand it over to him. "You, uh, lost something earlier."

He rips it from my hands, unfolding it with wide eyes. "This is confidential information. This letter is for my eyes only, do you understand!?"

"Well maybe you shouldn't leave it on the floor for the public's prying eyes."

Dreyden paces the room in a circle, unsure of how to react to all of this.

"Who are they? The Forces?"

He cautiously walks towards me, taking my hand. "You really want to know?"

I nod.

He nods in response. "Okay, but stay sitting down. This could take a while."

———

"You have to swear not to tell anyone."

"I swear." My heart starts palpitating.

"I am only telling you this because you deserve to know."

"Well, thanks in advance."

He sighs, then starts to talk. "We don't know who they are, specifically. But they're coming; they're coming for us all.

"It began with the genocide in Sudan in 2003. Our president at the time decided not to get involved—we weren't allies. Up until 2015, the attackers, who we now refer to as 'The Forces,' stayed only in that area. However, the group of rebels kept growing massively, until the attacks weren't targeted only at Sudan, but at the rest of the world. They got tired of the democratic, peaceful governments. They wanted the power to themselves. Our current president decided to keep quiet about it—it's best not to start a war unless absolutely necessary. In 2016, however, he decided to get a little experimental; to start preparing for the war before it even happened. The world is going up in flames, but America is not going with it.

"The most intellectual brains of science were brought together to create what is known as 'The New Awakening.' Humans, not yet fully developed, were injected with serums that supposedly form superhuman qualities. The serums took about a year to perfect. When the humans are born, or when they "awaken," the chemicals in the serums are already active and have formed and grown along with the natural development. It is suspected that by the time the human reaches the age of sixteen, their powers will have reached maximum evolution.

"The mother giving birth to the child has to give permission to sacrifice her life before we experiment with the child. The chemicals have to develop along with the child from their first sign of life, or else an unfamiliar reaction will be created, which is almost always fatal to the mother. After the mother dies, the child is given to scientists, where he or she will be raised thinking they are with their natural mother and father, while the "parents" keep track of the child's progression until sixteen years is up. Then, the child is off to the labs to be tested."

It is much too difficult to comprehend what I have just been told.

But whatever it is, it sounds like I'm in for quite a bit of crap. How lovely.

***

I can't sleep.

Dreyden's words circulate through my head in an endless loop. I have so many questions, but the answers seem to be drifting farther and farther away from me, like a boat astray at sea. When my eyes finally close, my imagination takes over, and a hazy image forms.

I see a woman. Her features are strikingly similar to mine; auburn hair cascades down her back, a few strands framing her olive complexion and green eyes. The setting is strange. Everything appears to be very outdated, like what we see in our history books. She is sitting in what I would guess is a waiting room, until she stands at the sound of a name being called: Jane.

A doctor takes her hand and leads her into a smaller, private room.

Once they're both seated, he starts speaking. "Tell me, Jane. Why do you want to be considered for this project?"

She clears her throat. "My husband was a soldier. He died two weeks ago trying to fight these people. I don't want anyone else to go through what he faced. I don't want anyone else to go through what I faced. I'm willing to do anything to make that happen." She wipes a tear from the corner from her eye, and sets a hand on her a stomach. "If my child has the same passion and audacity as my husband did, then—" She chokes back a sob. "My child should be able to fight these people, and win. At the very least, die trying."

The doctor seems to be taking this information in. "And you do know the sacrifice this involves, correct?"

She nods. "My life is of mere importance. My child's life is worth much more. I want my child to have an impact on this world. To thrive in the universe they are given."

He sighs. "Okay. We only have fourteen slots left of the former five thousand. Are you sure you want this?"

"I've never been more sure of anything."

"Alright. We'll meet in the operating room at ten tomorrow night." He stands and shakes her hand. "Oh, a couple more questions. How long has the child been in the womb?"

"About three weeks."

"Perfect. And you do have the option of choosing his/her name. Would you like to choose the name?"

"Yes, I would very much." Jane sits down once more, her kind eyes swimming with thought.

"Ever."

"Excuse me?"

"I want my child to be named Ever. It can work for a male or female. I don't want them to have a boring name like Jane. My child's legacy will live on, forever and ever. Their name needs to live up to that standard."

He hugs her. "I'm sure that will be nothing but true."

The next image I see will haunt me for years to come. Jane is lying on an operating table, her skin transparent and eyes lolled in the back of her head. Nurses are stuffing her into a body bag. One doctor is holding a baby girl, with flaming red hair and the greenest eyes I've ever seen. He walks into a room filled with baby cribs, and places her in a pink one with a sign labeled: Ever.

I wake up.

———

When Dreyden walks into my room, I am wallowing in a pile of dampened tissues. Very attractive, I'm sure.

"What's going on? Are you hurt?"

I can't bring myself to say the words. "Did you—did you know her?"

"Know who?"

"Jane."

A look of understanding washes over his face. "How do you know about Jane?"

I finger through my ponytail, brushing the tangles loose. "I had this dream. This woman, Jane; she gave birth to a daughter. A daughter named Ever."

"I see."

"Except—it sounded like what you were talking about earlier, with the chemical development, and with the mothers sacrificing their lives. That's what Jane did. She died, so her daughter could live and change the world."

"Interesting."

"Yes... Is she my real birth mother, Dreyden? And my real birth father, did he die in war?"

Dreyden shuffles towards the door. "That information is hidden in confidential files."

Now I'm angry. "I deserve to know who my real parents are, Dreyden. I deserve to know whether I am one of the Awakened. I deserve to know my entire life has been a lie!"

"According to the government, all you 'deserve' is to be locked in this room until further instruction."

"Go to Hell!"

"I'm afraid it's already occupied by you and your desire of the truth."

"I will break you."

"Yet I'm not the one in a mental institution, you are."

Satisfied, he exits. At first, I thought he was on my side. Now, he's just like all the other people of authority around here; making us patients feel inferior with their knowledge of our past, and our future.

———

Alarms sound throughout the entire building. Shouting. Screaming. The sound of shattering glass.

Just another beautiful evening.

I walk towards the door and begin to push the handle, but it doesn't budge. I try again; nothing.

I peer out of the shame of a window I have, and all I see are red, flashing lights. I'm going to go insane if I don't find out what's going on.

My eyes scan the room, until I find and open a drawer labeled *Emergency Tools*. Yes! A syringe with a needle! The needle easily breaks through the window glass, and I manage to climb out and get a good look at my surroundings.

Just follow the crowd. Easy.

I follow the trail of debris and blood, making sure not to step on any broken glass or nails. Then more obstacles appear. Bodies, nurses, oozing blood from the backs of their heads. It looks like a scene from a war.

Everyone is rushing outside into the night. I follow suit. It's the best experience I've had in a long, long time. Fresh air surrounds me, and I gaze at the stars hanging peacefully in the sky; a sight I've been longing for forever since my world flipped upside down.

And then the gunshots go off, and reality smacks me in the face once more. This is my world now. A world of bitter survival, leaning on a wall of truths strung together by lies. Instead of raindrops, bullets fall from the sky. Instead of sunshine, the tragedies of our pasts shimmer on our souls. This is my world now, and I better get used to it.

I see her! Platinum Woods, the girl I've been yearning to find and take vengeance, is climbing on top of the roof of the institution! Suddenly, I don't care about the fact that Wren kissed her. She is my link to all of this madness. She knows the truth. I must reach her.

But I'm too late. A bullet soars towards her, piercing her skull. She falls down, down, down. Until I hear this sound, this horrific sound that echoes so loud, everyone in existence had to have heard it. Everyone falls into silence, as if mourning the awful incident we had to witness.

I collapse on the cement and sob, as my world begins to spin and doesn't stop.

***

I'm breathing.

I'm conscious in my room, and air is going in and out through my lungs. My heart is pumping blood through my veins. I have survived. I am alive.

The last memory I can recall before I lost consciousness was Wren. I remember seeing him scream as she fell, punching the guards amidst his lunacy. I was crying and then everything went black.

I find it absolutely incredible how in a few measly weeks, society has gone haywire and every single person, and I mean *every human* in existence, seems to have lost their minds.

When I finally work up the courage to open my eyes, he's there.

"We need to talk."

"Oh, is there a problem? My goodness, what could it be?" I could play this game with Dreyden all night long if I had to.

"I don't have time for any of it, Ever. What you witnessed out there…" he gulped, avoiding my gaze. "You need to forget it happened. Do you understand me?"

"No, I don't." This made me all the more confused. "Why should I forget it happened? An innocent girl was shot, Dreyden! Maybe what she did was against the rules, but frankly, I'm about to go insane in here, too! You see, here's the thing, pal. If you take people from their homes, deprive them from any contact to the outside world, and keep them locked in a fucking cell without a clear explanation, then you can NOT expect those people to do what you say. You cannot expect them to obey your every command, as if they're your servants. You cannot control people's lives!"

"I'm not trying to control your life! You don't get it, Ever!" He looks like a deer in the headlights. He's sweating bullets, and his eyes are wide and filled with fear. It's scaring me. "You don't understand all the chaos going on around you. Seven people died in the time span it took me to say that sentence." He finally lets out a breath, slow, but angry. "You don't know shit. So please, I am begging you, forget what you saw!"

The tears start, though I try and hold them in. "Fine! Maybe I don't know shit! But I do know one thing. If we're all going to die, I certainly don't wanna do it in this hell hole!"

I stalk out of my room and into the woman's bathroom, the one place I can be alone.

And then it hits me. I have no one.

This time I can't ignore the excruciating pain. It curls around my joints, ceasing their movement. It twists my thoughts and words, jumbling them into nonsensical gibberish. It wraps around my lungs, squeezing them to the point where I can no longer breathe. Once your heart has been shattered time and time again, your fate, too, seems irreparable. There's no way to express within a combination of twenty-six letters how broken I feel.

I cannot begin to comprehend the idea of continuing this life. What purpose is there, to live in a mindset of agony such as my own? I am no longer in a state of being, but a state of dying; I might as well speed up the process.

God, I'm such an idiot! How could I have been so damn foolish? When I was younger, fairytale books in preschool were my only source of literature. I was taught to follow unrealistic faith, no matter how absurd. I wore my heart on my sleeve, blindly giving it to every person I was ever close too. I should've known the outcome. I threw a piece of glass into an abyss, expecting it to remain intact; if that isn't utter stupidity, I don't know what is.

But still—you try so hard to find people. People who accept you, flaws and all. People you can lean on in your darkest hours. And among them, you wish to find this person, this person who was created for you and only you to cherish. They were to be your everlasting soulmate. You connected emotionally, drawn together by your relentless passions that no other two people in the world deem as worthy. Though as usually to no avail, you're stuck pondering the idea whether soulmates exist at all, and if love is just a crazy concept we're all chasing after and yearning to catch.

Or maybe I'm the crazy one for ever believing love existed.

I finally seek out Dreyden again. I just had to clear my head and keep my thoughts on track. It's hard, though, finding a reason to live.

He's down the hall in one of the offices. I can hear his voice. He sounds like he's on the telephone.

I quietly approach the room to eavesdrop. They're speaking in a language I can't make out. My foreign language classes come into use, though, and I catch a few key points:

"She's… health well… tools…useful… must keep safe…"

When I hear the resigning sound of the dial tone, I begin to confront him in person.

"So, who was that on the phone?"

Dreyden grins. "Hey, Ever. You doing better?"

"Who was that on the phone?"

"Didn't I just tell you to stay out my business?"

"Was the 'she' reference about me?"

His eyes go wide once more, and he scares me again. "Exactly how much of that could you interpret?"

"Not a lot."

"Good. And no, I was not referring to you."

"Well, good."

But it appears to be the opposite of good. Dreyden hides out all day, constantly on the phone, speaking in languages I have no knowledge of. He stays quiet and under the radar, as if something bad will happen if he speaks to anybody directly. My curiosity, of course, gets the best of me.

When he walks to the phone room, I follow about fifty feet behind him. Whatever he's keeping secret, I'm going to find out what it is.

Who knows; he knew about The New Awakening, what other knowledge does he have of America's past?

But I never reach the door. A shady figure is sprinting toward me. I cannot make out any of the shadow's features. They reach out. They grab me. I scream...

Up until the duct tape seals my mouth shut.

Part 3

Hendrix

He's coming.

I hear his footsteps, thumping so heavily they're shaking the foundation of the house. There's no way I can escape. Not this time.

I can feel his presence lurking near my door.

I tried using my wooden desk chair as a lever against the doorknob. It will cause little resistance, if any. I've seen him kick down doors before. Hell, I've seen him kick holes through walls.

And now he's coming, and there's nothing I can do to stop him.

I'm okay, though. If he hit any of the girls I'd kill him, but he only targets me. If he harms any one of them, though, I'll take out the six-inch switch blade I've had stored in my boot since I was ten and I'll slit his throat.

"Hendrix!" his gravelly voice ricochets off the walls. "I think it's time I taught you a lesson, don't you?"

It was only one dollar. Aaron and Howie were heading up to the new club to flirt with college girls, and I was only one dollar short of the entrance fee. So I stole one from his wallet.

I should've known he'd find out. And I should've known he'd react this way.

"Would you like to come out here, or should I go in there?"

Here it comes.

His foot breaks down the door, the hinges soaring above my head. The situation vaguely reminds me of a stanza from the poem "Song of Myself" by Walt Whitman. "Unscrew the locks from the door! Unscrew the doors themselves from their jambs!"

The five o'clock shadow on his chin gives him a tough appearance. Beads of sweat run down his forehead, soaking the thin cloth of his tattered t-shirt. None of this fazes me, though; it's his eyes. They are hard and cold, ruthless tunnels of despair.

"WHY THE HELL DID YOU STEAL MY MONEY!?"

I stumble backward in shock. I've never heard him scream this loud before. It's terrifying. Dread creeps up my spine.

"I told you NEVER to touch my stuff! Damnit, Hendrix, are you deaf!? Do you need to go to school for dumb asses!? Huh, is that what you need!?"

"I'm sorry."

"What did you just say!? You're SORRY? Ha ha ha! That's hilarious, son! So *fucking* hilarious! You should be a comedian!"

"Demarcus, stop harassing our son."

I spin around and see my mother. Her usually kind eyes are filled with worry, and she has tears running down her face. I absolutely hate seeing my mother cry. She doesn't deserve this.

"Mom," I whisper. "Please go away. I'm handling this."

She wraps her arms around me. "You have no right to be treated like this."

She turns towards him. "I'm calling the police, Demarcus. You need some serious help."

"You're the one who needs help, Eileen!" Suddenly, his hand makes contact with her face, and I hear a painful sound I've heard so many times, it's unmistakable.

He hit her. He hit my mother.

Nobody hits my mother.

"Hey, asshole!" I'm about ready to take out my switchblade, but he stalks away, and I spot the girls right behind me. They look scared, but Emmaline the worst of all. She's only five. She can't watch this.

I shove the blade back in my boot. "Hey girls." I gather them in a hug. "Go back to your rooms, okay? Nothing to worry about. Sweet dreams."

They follow in a line back to their bedrooms, all but Aoife.

"Were you... were you going to kill him?"

I look into her eyes, a dark shade of violet, just like mine. I've been her father figure all her life, since Demarcus clearly was not. She knows of everything. But she's still filled with youth and innocence, and I do not want to destroy that purity. I don't want her turning into myself at the age of twelve.

"No. It's okay. You're okay."

She nods.

"Hen... I just want you to know, that even if you did—" she gulps. "I wouldn't be sad."

She buries her head into my chest, and I stroke her hair. "Twinkle, twinkle, what do I spy? I spy Aoife in the sky."

She giggles the same giggle she's had since she was a year old. When she was little, she'd cry non-stop, except whenever I'd hum that song to her. Then she'd fall asleep in my arms, and I would rock her until she awoke.

"Off to bed, now."

Once she scampered off, I took to my mother's bedroom. This has to end right now.

I find her sitting in bed, tissues surrounding her. Her eyes are red, like she's been sobbing.

"Mom? Where is he?"

She barely manages to choke words out. "He's in his room." Her hands reach out for me. "Are you hurt?"

"No, I'm fine." I sit beside her and rub her back. "Mom," Inhale. Exhale. "I need you to take the girls and get out of here."

She turns towards me. "What? Honey, what are you talking about? I'm not going to run away, especially not without you."

"No. That's not what I meant." I exit the room and come back with a suitcase. "This has all the basic necessities. One thousand dollars, a week's worth of clothing, toiletries, a supply of food, and a gun."

I see the look on her face. She thinks I'm crazy. "Hendrix, what are you saying? We're just going to take off in the middle of the night? You know he'll find us!"

"Go to the nearest hotel and book a room, at least for the night. It's two in the morning right now. I'll be there by six." I kiss her cheek. "Mom, it's not safe here. Not for you, me, the girls… we need to get out of here before he really hurts one of us."

All the color has drained from her face. I feel bad for asking this from her, but it's the only way we have the opportunity for a better life. A life without him in it.

She nods. "Okay." Her hand takes mine. "Okay. We'll be out of the house in thirty minutes."

I stay hidden in my room until I'm positive they've left. Then, it begins.

I've been planning this for about two and a half years. I realized that if I tried to kill him with my switchblade, his reflexes would be quicker and I'd end up dead on the floor instead of him. A gun wouldn't work either; my shot isn't that great.

But there aren't any rules against playing with fire.

I take the gun powder I'd been secretly saving and cautiously spread it out on the wooden floor. My lighter, which I haven't put to use since I was thirteen and Howie dared me to smoke a cigarette, finally becomes valuable. I am prepared to run.

And when the flame ignites, I run like I never have before.

Barely after the flame is lit, I can feel the heat quickly absorb into my bones. Orange and red dance before my eyes, blurring my vision. I have to get out of here. Smoke fills my lungs, and I dodge falling timber.

I'm about to exit the doorway until I see my book sitting on the foyer table. I quickly shove it in my back pocket and break free from the house. I spin around to watch the flames eat it alive. But then I hear something.

"Hawk!"

When Emmaline was first born, everyone had called me Hen, short for Hendrix. However, she thought that was too feminine, and that my nickname should be Hawk instead, since "that's what boy birds are called." She loved calling me that. She thought she was special, since she was the only one who used it.

So when I heard a tiny voice scream "Hawk!" I knew it wasn't my father.

It was Emmaline.

It's all too surreal. My skin tightens and jaw clenches and head spins and throat closes and I can't comprehend the thought of what I just did...

I want to cry, but no tears come out.

Suddenly, the gun powder truly reacts. An explosion, unlike any other, shatters the house to pieces.

The last thing I see before my vision cuts off is a body—a small, fragile body. It lands approximately fifteen feet from where I'm standing, and I don't dare look at the face.

I can't.

***

The smell of burning firewood rises into my nostrils, and for a second, I still believe I'm at the scene. I jolt awake and gradually realize I'm no longer at the house, but in the middle of a forest. I believe it's the Ferncliff Forest; I went camping here with friends a long time ago. Draped over my body is a blanket weaved together by foliage and spider silk. I can only assume it's what kept me warm throughout the night.

My book! I reach for the back pocket of my jeans, which are covered with ash, and begin to panic. It's gone. I sink to the forest floor and curl in a ball. It was my most treasured possession.

"Hey, Sleeping Beauty's awake!"

A woman stands in front of me. Right away, I can tell she's not someone you mess around with. Her wild brown curls are cropped short, just below her chin. She has fiery hazel eyes with a glimmer of mischief swirling within them.

And in her right hand is my book.

She smirks. "Yeah, I thought I'd give it a go. You're pretty deep for a dude. Don't find many people like that in West Lake."

She hands it over to me with callused fingers, and I get a good look at her t-shirt. It reads 'Cardinal Sin'.

"Jonterri Gadson."

"What?"

"Your shirt. There's a poem called "Cardinal Sin" by Jonterri Gadson."

"Yeah. I really like her work."

"How come?"

She seems reluctant at first, but then speaks. "That poem in particular is about a mother failing her children, but instead of trying to fix the problem, she lives in denial. That's how my mother raised me."

I feel as if I've invaded her privacy. "Oh."

"So, you're pretty into poetry." She nods toward my book. "You write?"

"A little."

"I liked the one called 'Faded.' Can you read it to me?"

I feel my cheeks blush. Nobody had ever read these poems except for me. "I don't even know your name."

She smiles. "Cleo. I'm seventeen. How about you?"

"Hendrix. Hendrix Asher. I'm sixteen."

"Hendrix. That's way too formal. You got any nicknames?"

"Ah," I get a feeling of discomfort. "Hawk. My nickname's Hawk."

"Radical. You wanna know something else radical?"

"I'm not sure…"

"Yeah you do. Get some confidence, pal, or you're never gonna survive out here. My actual name's Cleodora, but that name's freakin ancient, so I changed it to Cleo when I was nine years old. It's stuck ever since."

"Oh. Cool."

"Eh. Compared to everything else cool in the world, like skydiving or discovering an alternative universe, shortening your name is probably on the low-end of the cool scale."

"Yeah…"

"So, Hawk, care to read me your poem?"

"I guess."

I open my book, and turn through the pages until I find the right one. Cleo stares at me, intrigued, and when I begin to read, she shuts her eyes.

"No longer do I wince from scars, but memories.

Looming o'er the joyous rays

Showering o'er with twisted pain.

And I ponder each return

With great curiosity:

What pleasure does he receive?

Besides the illusion of vengeance

And the trickery of supremacy?

For they are faded,

But I continue to see."

Cleo finally opens her eyes and studies me. I notice that behind the glimmer of mischief they behold, they are kind, and also broken.

"Please tell me what it is about."

I play with the ends of my shirt, hesitant. It's too personal. "It's about my father. He abused me and my family."

"Abused? As in past tense?"

"I killed him last night."

The reality finally strikes me. I killed my father. You'd figure I'd be overjoyed, but I'm not. I feel numb.

"Is that why you started writing poetry? To have a place where you can put your thoughts into words?"

She stole the words right from my mouth. I nod. "Yes."

Cleo comes towards me and hugs me. It's funny. I don't know her, and I don't know where I am or how I got here, but she is the first person I could ever tell any of that to without feeling afraid or foolish.

Actually, it's not funny. It's sad.

I pull away from her. "Can I ask you something?"

"Of course."

"Where am I?"

And just to make things all the more confusing, someone appears behind her. "C'mon, Cleo. If you don't hurry up, I'm feeding your breakfast to the squirrels."

"So, this is the new kid?"

Cleo glares at him. "Shut your mouth, Vin. He's useful." She shoves more deer meat into her mouth, and I struggle not to heave.

The guy strokes his shaggy, greasy hair. The constant stroking is starting to annoy me. "I'm Vinny, by the way; Cleo's brother. We're exactly five minutes apart."

It doesn't surprise me that they're twins, seeing as their features are so similar. Like Cleo, Vinny also has curly brown hair and hazel eyes, as well as a tan complexion. He's very tall, too. If I had to guess, probably 6'7. I'm only 5'11, which is embarrassing, considering Cleo's only two inches shorter.

"Yup," Cleo pats him on the back. "Cleodora and Vincent. Our parents definitely deserve an award for choosing the worst possible names to name your children."

I crack a smile. I enjoy Cleo's humor.

Vinny clears his throat. "So, Hawk. Tell me a little about yourself. Why are you here with us?"

I'm about to speak, but Cleo interrupts me. "Hawk is a deep dude. He writes poetry. He comes from an abusive father. And he's here because he can help us."

"I can help you with what?"

Vinny lowers his eyes. "Stopping them."

"Who?"

"The Forces."

***

"You're one of us."

I still don't understand. "Who's *us*?"

The two share a look of concern and pity, as if what they're about to tell me is somewhat of a burden. "The Awakened."

"Well, yeah… I'm pretty sure all of us are awake currently…" I'm still in a state of bewilderment.

Cleo's eyes light up for a moment, but then the light is gone. "It's too difficult to explain at the moment." She rises from her log and starts to walk away, but I stop her. I'm not finished. "I want to know."

Vinny's glare pierces through mine. "Look, kid. You're not ready. Not yet, at least. Let's just say without us, you're gonna die, so if I were you, I'd stick with us and don't ask a lot of questions."

I try and sustain what little patience I have left. "I need to find my mom and sisters. I don't have time for any of this crap."

"You can't."

"Why not?"

"Because," Cleo rubs her forehead, and for once I see stress swirling within the humor in her eyes. "I'm not exactly sure yet, but I'm pretty sure you're in a state of quintessence. It can be slightly common for those who are of our kind."

"What is that? What is *quintessence*?"

Vinny rolls his eyes. "Ah, so you're a newbie at this. Jeez, kid, have you been living under a rock your whole life?"

"It means that your body has experienced severe damage, some even beyond repair. Your mind is still in full function, even if your body is not. In some extremely rare cases, the mind takes this wasted energy and transforms it into what is known as your spirit."

"Excuse me?"

Cleo takes my hand. "Everyone has their own spiritual self. It usually doesn't activate until your earth form dies, but your case is a bit different than any normal human; which is why we know you're one of The Awakened."

My mind is swimming, and I become dizzy. "So, what you're saying is, I'm not human right now; I'm some sort of spirit?"

"Exactly."

"And how do you know this?"

"Because currently your body is in a coma in the local hospital."

This is impossible. This goes way beyond any sense of moral logic... I don't believe it. I can't believe it. "That's crazy. This whole thing is insane. I'm sorry to be so abrupt, but I have to leave and find my family."

"There's no chance of that happening." Vinny stands up and spits into the fire, and I watch it turn to ashes. "Your mom and three of your sisters are off the grid, and your father and Emmaline are dead."

Dead. The word punches me in the face, and sparks of pain and grief spread throughout my body. "That's not true."

I am testing Vinny's patience. I can see it in his eyes. "Yeah it is, so get used to it."

Cleo turns towards me. "We're not making this up, Hawk. I know it's unbelievable and I know it's dangerous and complicated and the whole thing sucks, but trust us. Trust ME. I want you to close your eyes and envision yourself in your body. You'll see the truth."

"I still don't understand though. What is The Awakened, and why am I part of it?"

Cleo gives me a sad smile. "No one knows why we were chosen. If I explain the whole of it to you, you will go into a state of shock. It's too much for the human brain to comprehend within a short period of time. For right now, please close your eyes, and imagine yourself in your body."

I surrender and do as I'm told.

Something weird happens. A blast of cold air shoots through my veins, and I struggle to inhale oxygen. Then the pain comes. It's unlike anything I've experienced before. I try to fight it, try to escape the pain, but my fists and legs are tied together. Finally, my eyes pop open. I catch a glimpse of a hospital.

"EMMALINE!"

Like a bullet, the name shoots from my throat until my lungs burn. I can't gather my thoughts together, though. My mind replays her body flying through the air again and again as she is thrown from the explosion. It is a sick and tragic film I do not want to watch.

The pain comes to a rest, as I jolt awake with Cleo and Vinny towering over me.

"Are you okay?" I realize I'm now lying on the ground. I touch my head, and my hand comes away wet and smeared with red.

"Here, that should stop the bleeding." Vinny tosses me a roll of toilet paper, and I wrap it around my head until I'm left with just the cardboard roll.

"What happened to me?"

Cleo looks at me with pity. "You were screaming gibberish, and you started running until you ran into a tree, then you fell."

I reluctantly stand, testing my balance. "Okay. So what do we do now?"

Vinny throws his arm around me. "You get to meet the others."

We trek a long way down a dirt road for about thirty-five minutes. I chat with Cleo and Vinny, and it's kind of nice. I'm still deeply confused, but I lay off the questions for a while and decide to relax. It's a refreshing sense of relief. Then I hear laughter; actual laughter. It's music to my ears.

Up ahead, I wince at the sight of a great fire sizzling in the center of an abandoned parking lot. People ranging from their young teens to late twenties are dancing and grinning. Kids throw their heads back mid-chuckle, telling jokes with their friends. A couple is slow dancing, despite the upbeat music playing in the background. They secretly smile to each other, as if they are the only two people in the world. My parents used to be like that.

"What is this place?"

Vinny smiles a devilish grin. 'This, my friend, is The Lot; AKA where your life begins. Every night, people of our kind gather here and party."

"Which basically means drinking booze and hooking up; you feel like crap the next day, but it sure as hell feels good at night!" Cleo laughs at her own comment, and I laugh with her.

"What do you mean 'our kind'?"

"Everyone else who is part of The Awakened. Again, we'll explain all that later, but it's your first night with us; let loose and have a good time. We'll catch up with you later!" They run off and join a mob of other teenagers, who welcome them with open arms.

"Wait!" I'm debating whether I should follow or not, when a voice comes at me from behind.

"Hey, your friends ditch you?"

I spin around and meet the owner of the voice. She's wearing a blue and white striped top that cuts off just above her belly button, and shows off all of her curves. Her jeans flare at the ankles, and underneath are leather boots with a small heel to them. Her blonde hair goes all the way down to her hips. Her teeth are chattering, but her green eyes are warm and friendly.

"Aren't your freezing? It's like thirty degrees out here; I'm surprised it isn't snowing." It looks like that's about to change, however, judging from the clouds.

"Yeah, a little." She giggles, and I take off my jacket, but she shakes her head.

"No, I'm fine. I'm used to it, really."

"Please, take it."

"I'm fine! Sorry, I'm not trying to sound rude, but really, I'm good."

I smile. "You're okay. I'm Hendrix, by the way."

She smiles back. "Alia."

"That's a pretty name."

"Thank you. So, you're friends with Cleo and Vinny, yeah?"

I shrug. "Uh, yeah, sorta."

"Yeah, makes sense."

"What do you mean?"

She rolls her eyes. "Duh, Cleo's hot. Every guy in the universe wants to be friends with Cleo, but she only befriends the ones who are also equally attractive as her. So, doesn't surprise me."

I laugh. "That's insane."

"Not really. You're a solid nine, maybe a nine-point-five on a good day; especially with those purple eyes and that shiny black hair of yours. You're also pretty ripped. She'll hook up with you eventually."

"So, she just hooks up with any guy who's hot?"

"Yup, she's known for her spunk outside and inside the bedroom." Alia winks at me.

"I can't believe you just said that!" I burst into laughter.

"I speak the truth, my man." She grins. "You wanna get some hot chocolate?"

"Sure."

I spend the rest of the night with Alia by my side. I don't touch one drop of alcohol or hook up with anyone, but I don't need that to have a good time. Alia tells me of her hilarious childhood memories and most embarrassing moments, and suddenly we're no longer strangers but lifelong friends. When darkness takes over, everyone dances in the snowflakes as they fall.

Maybe things are starting to look up. Maybe I've found where I belong.

Maybe I'm finally home.

***

My bones are frigid.

I open my eyes, and realize I'm lying on the asphalt in The Lot. One of my arms is draped over Alia's stomach. Her blonde hair glistens in the early morning light, and I sweep it away from her face to see her eyes shut. She's still asleep.

When I finally get up, relief washes over me. We're not the only ones who fell asleep in the midst of all the fun. Dozens of people are scattered across the asphalt, some clothed, some not, but asleep nonetheless.

I look back at Alia once more. She's so peaceful. I take out my book from my jeans pocket and write on a blank page: *The girl with the long blonde hair*. A good start to a poem.

 I turn to leave, and I gradually find my way back to Cleo and Vinny's campground.

"Aye, Hawk, you're back!" Vinny's roasting some sort of meat above a small fire. It smells delicious, and my hunger gets to me. All I've eaten in the last 48 hours is a cup of hot chocolate and some crackers.

"Can I, uh, have some of that?" I say hesitantly.

Vinny nods. "Yeah, sure! My buddy Reed scored some beef and gave us a hunk of it. It was a good thing, 'cuz I was gettin' sick of that old deer meat!"

"Okay, thanks."

He smirks. "So, Alia Wordsworth, huh? She's got a decent face, but she doesn't really have much of a rack, if you know what I mean. Then again, you're new here, so you probably just jumped on the first chick that approached you."

He winks, and I'm so indignant I'm not even sure how to respond. "I didn't 'jump' on anyone. She's nice to talk to, so we chatted for a while. We didn't make out or anything."

"Ah, okay, whatever you say pal. Listen, if you're looking for a good time, though, I'd recommend getting with Petal Bloomington. She's got the name of a stripper, and her body looks like a Photoshopped model on the cover of a magazine. And, she's bisexual, so she'll do it with boys and girls, which I think is pretty sexy if you ask me."

"Uh, I'm good." Vinny and I have different definitions of "a good time."

"Hawk!" Cleo runs up from behind me and hugs me. Her caramel-colored curls are sticking up in every direction, and her eyes are sparkly and filled with wonder. "Sorry I wasn't back earlier. I fell asleep in The Lot last night. Did you have a good time?"

"Yeah, I did."

"Cool. Who'd you talk to?"

"This girl named Alia. She has really long blonde hair, kinda short—"

"Ew, her? Sorry to say, Hawk, but she's a complete outcast. She's really lonely and weird. I have some cute friends who are totally interested in you, though, so we can sort that out later."

"Oh. Okay."

She nods and grins. "Well, I'm gonna go out fishing. Wanna come with, Vin?"

"Sure." He stands up and brushes his pants off. "Keep watch over the fort, Hawk. We'll be back in an hour or so."

Once they're gone, I hear a rustling in a nearby bush. I swivel around, only to find a pair of bright green eyes meeting mine.

"Alia?"

She shows herself. "I need to talk to you."

As we walk and her fingers pick out stray leaves from the ends of her hair, she speaks. "What have they told you?"

"Told me what?"

"About your reason for being here?"

I gulp. "Uh, nothing really."

"That's what I thought." She pauses mid-step.

"Okay, I know what you're thinking. This is a fun place, a place where everyone lives in harmony and everything's awesome and wild. That's not true. Those are lies. This place, it's a place for people, people like us, to temporarily run away from their problems. Where we can escape the reality of the true Hell we're living in."

"Why does everyone keeping classifying 'us' as some sort of hybrid species?"

"Because that's what we are."

"What are you talking about?" She's starting to scare me.

Alia puts her hands on my shoulders. "We are The Awakened. We are the offspring who have been perfected and modified to fit the standards of the ultimate soldier. Eventually, we will be placed in a war, a war nobody has won—yet. Our mothers sacrificed their lives, so that when we Awoke, we could make an impact in the war. They thought we could stop it for good." She sits down on the forest floor. "My mother died so that I could take vengeance for my father's death. And here I am, hiding out from the government and trying to avoid the Placement Process, making her sacrifice worth nothing!" Alia sobs.

I hug her. "I still don't understand."

She looks up at me, her eyes pooling with mist. "You are also born with this burden. I encourage you to run, to get out of here as fast as you can. The president is onto us, he knows some of his captives are running loose, and he is going to find our location sooner or later. Not only will we be punished, but we will still end up getting Placed. Get out of here."

"No, I'm not going to just leave! If I'm carrying this burden, I'm going to make it worth something. I want you tell me the truth; what have I been blinded from all these years?"

Alia doesn't meet my gaze. "'The Forces' is their code name. They're like tyrants, committing all these mass killings unceasingly. It's incredible, really. Our president knew they would eventually make their way here, so he made us. He combined all these genes to create super humans, and those super humans are us. We're immune to things a majority of people aren't, and our neurological power is significantly higher than most. Anyway, in order for this to work, the mother carrying the embryo had to give up her life, because the chemical reaction would be too strong for her body to sustain. Whoever you lived with before were not your biological parents. Most of the mothers who volunteered had husbands who were soldiers—husbands who died while fighting The Forces. My mother wrote me this letter before she died, telling me that she was counting on me to be a hero."

"Isn't that a good thing?"

"No, that's a burden! What if I don't want to fight the war? What if I want to live out a normal life? I know, that's so selfish, but I'm not a hero. I'm not a hero!" She smacks the ground.

I don't know what to say. "What do I do?"

Alia finally looks at me. "You run. You run, and you never look back."

***

"You've got to be kidding me. Hawk, buddy, listen to me. She's mentally unstable. She's got no clue what she's talking about, just filling your brain with nonsense crap."

"Then what *is* she talking about?" Alia couldn't have just made that all up off the top of her head.

Cleo shakes her head. "Nothing important. I don't want you hanging around her anymore, though. She's not good for you. Now, Vin and I are going out drinking. You comin' or what?"

"Can't you just wait till sunset, when we head over to The Lot?"

She grins a sly smile. "It's five o'clock somewhere! See ya later, Hawk." She runs off with two gorgeous women, and I listen to their laughter slowly fade.

"Hendrix!" Alia jumps out from a nearby tree.

I'm taken aback. "Jeez, you've got to quit doing that! You'll end up giving me a heart attack!"

She giggles profusely. "I'm sorry, but if Cleo caught me on her territory, she'd freak."

"Why is that exactly? She doesn't seem to have a liking towards you."

Alia shrugs. "She's a sweetheart to those who are of her same status. If you're not, like *moi*, she can be a complete bitch."

"Wait, what do you mean by status?"

"If we were in a school, she'd be in what you call the popular crowd."

"Oh."

"Oh indeed." She steps towards me. "I came here because I wanted to show you something."

I follow her through a hidden pathway. We don't say much, but I think it's because we're both so mesmerized by the beauty of the wildlife around us. Leaves made of emerald twinkle with droplets of snowflakes, and the crisp air is refreshing, like nature's morning breath. The moon is out early; it stares down at us with a loving gaze. I take out my book once more, and write.

"What's that?"

"This? Oh, nothing."

"Clearly it's something." Alia twirls one of her long golden braids around her finger. "I wanna see it."

"Not… yet."

She smiles, but doesn't press me anymore. We continue on our journey, until we come to a stop at a large structure.

The bricks are a deep crimson, covered in dust and wearing dozens of cobwebs. The entrance doors are grand and were clearly once magnificent, but they too are run-down; a faded navy blue, chipped at the edges. The atmosphere is very eerie, and I am apprehensive about whatever Alia's plotting.

"What is this place? Are we allowed to be in here?"

"This," Alia gestures, "is called a library."

A feeling of familiarity comes over me. "Oh, right! People used to come to these for books and research."

"Exactly." She nods. "This is also where you're going to meet your parents for the first time."

———

Alia clicks away at the ancient computer, despite my trying to stop her.

"You're absolutely insane. There's no way there's going to be any record of my parents, and even if there was, I don't want to know!" Ever since she told me the truth behind my past, I've gradually began to feel the same burden she's described. When your parents sacrifice their lives for your ability to make a difference in the world, you don't really realize the pressure until it smacks you in the face one day.

That day, for me, is today.

Alia gasps, and her green eyes widen. "I've got it. Come here, look at this."

I walk over next to her and glance over her shoulder. A photo appears. It's in color, but the quality isn't very good.

I see a man. He has black hair, like mine, and steely grey eyes. He's very built, the opposite of my slim bone structure. He's handsome, but in a more brooding way. A woman stands next to him, her arms wrapped around his waist. She is very pretty. She too has black hair, but her eyes stand out. They are purple. A dark shade of violet, you might say.

Just like mine.

And that is when I know that these are, in fact, my biological parents.

Underneath the image, it says "William and Mary Asher, circa 1993. Ages: 17."

Wow. Almost forty years ago. Times have changed so much. I continue to read more facts as Alia scrolls down.

"Graduated: 1994.

Occupations: William was a soldier, Mary was a poet.

Date of death: 2016.

Children: Hendrix, currently 16.

Adopted Siblings: Merida, currently 14. Aoife, currently 12. Rita, currently 8. Emmaline, age 5 at time of death.

Adopted parents: Demarcus and Eileen Wethers.

Other History: William Asher died in war. Mary Asher died of unknown causes. After deaths, their only child, Hendrix, who was an infant at the time, was given to adopting parents Demarcus and Eileen.

Other News: Demarcus Wethers died last week in a house fire, as did one of Hendrix's adopted siblings, Emmaline. The cause of the fire is still to be determined, though it is suspected to be ignited by Hendrix himself. Hendrix is currently comatose, so no reassurance has been concluded."

I'm dizzy.

Alia turns to look at me, worry flashing in her eyes. "You killed your dad and sister?"

"Let's just go. I need to go."

I lean partially on Alia's shoulder as we walk out of the library. I can't seem to think. The quiet doesn't last for long, though. Black helicopters hover above us in the sky.

"Hendrix Asher, raise your arms!"

Terror pulses through my veins as a voice belts out orders at me. What's going on?

"I repeat, raise your arms! You're being taken under arrest!"

I do as I'm told.

I hear footsteps behind me, and spin around to see Cleo and Vinny. They are completely hungover, but their arms are cuffed behind them, and they're being escorted by two men in black.

"Vincent and Cleodora Edwards, you are being taken under arrest! You have the right to remain silent!" The helicopter slowly makes its descent onto the ground. Several men climb out, handcuffing the oblivious twins and shoving them into the doors of the helicopter. A man begins to cuff my hands as well, but I fight back.

"I didn't do anything wrong, sir!"

"You have an association with the Edwards twins; we're required to bring you in for questioning."

"What did they do?"

He looks at me, and I see the same terror in my eyes being reflected in his. "They are a part of The Forces."

***

A large steel door crashes behind me.

As directed, I sit across from a man who resembles what I had always imagined a spy would look like. Examining the room, I notice there are four cameras placed discreetly in each corner. Finally, the man clears his throat, and I do the same.

"Do you solemnly swear that you will tell the truth, the whole truth, and nothing but the truth, so help you God?"

"I solemnly swear that I will tell the truth, the whole truth, and nothing but the truth, so help me God."

"Please state your full name and date of birth."

"Hendrix William Asher, born January 23, 2016."

"How are you associated with Vincent Edwards?"

I can't answer this, at least not logically. "I was introduced to him by his sister just a few days ago."

"Would you say you are engaged in a friendly relationship with Mr. Edwards?"

"Yes, sir."

"Over the previous period of time, did you notice any suspicious activity from Mr. Edwards?"

"No, sir."

"Thank you for your honesty. How are you associated with Cleodora Edwards?"

Don't hesitate, or he'll think you're lying. "She took me in when I found myself in a desperate situation."

He raises his eyebrows. "How would you describe this situation?"

"I ran away from home."

"Why? Were you offered something from Miss Edwards, to draw you away from your home?"

No! "No, sir. My father and I had a fight."

"Were you in an abusive household?"

I gulp. "No sir."

"This was a verbal fight?"

"Yes sir."

"I see." He scribbled something down on his notepad. "Were you associated with Cleodora before this incident?"

"No sir, she was a complete stranger, until she found me in the woods and took me in."

"Would you say you are currently engaged in a friendly relationship with Miss Edwards?"

"Yes, sir."

"Were you ever in a sexual relationship?"

"No sir, we're only friends." That's awkward.

"Over the previous period of time, did you notice any suspicious activity from Miss Edwards?"

"No sir."

"Thank you for your honesty. As a result of their illegal scheming against the United States of America, your friends will soon be exterminated. The government appreciates your time, Mr. Asher, and we will get back to you shortly."

Exterminated. Cleo and Vinny are going to be *exterminated.* They're going to die.

"What? Why!? They didn't do anything wrong!" I stand up from my chair. "Punishment by death is only for serial killers or psychopaths!"

The guard stands up as well, making sure to show off his strength and authority as he does so. He grabs my shirt. "Listen here, kid. Your friends were planning to kill innocent citizens of America. I don't want that, and neither do you. They've been spying on this country for so long it's sickening. They deserve death. Sorry, Mr. Asher, but your friends are bad, bad people."

I am escorted back to a waiting room. I'm in a sort of stupor. Cleo and Vinny can't be who the government thinks they are. Cleo's the life of the party, and everyone loves her. And Vinny, he's so cool and relaxed. I can't imagine any of them wanting to take a person's life.

I guess I'd better get used to it; people hiding who they really are.

About a half hour later, a woman calls my name back into the questioning room. "Mr. Asher, I'm afraid you're going to have to be called into court."

"What?"

She avoids my glare. "The suspects have claimed that their best friend is Hawk, which from what we have concluded, is your nickname. This means you have quite a close correlation with the suspects. Also, your interview with one of our guards earlier provoked more questions, and some think that you too are involved with this plot."

"I swear I'm not! I just figured out who these Forces are a couple days ago!"

She raises an eyebrow. "Excuse me?"

"Never mind. Just, let me know when I need to come in."

"Sure thing."

I begin my trek back from the police station, trying to find my way back to the campgrounds. I cannot believe they think I'm guilty. I can't even remember how I was dragged into this. On my way back, however, I spot Alia. She's curled up near a tree, her blonde hair covering her face.

"Alia!" I start to jog towards her, but she stands up and backs away. Her eyes are swirling with fear, and she cowers behind the trunk of the tree.

"Stay away." She repeats, "Stay away from me!"

I'm stunned. "You don't actually believe I'm a part of this, do you? That I planned some massacre with Cleo and Vinny?"

She shakes her head. "I don't know what to believe anymore. They were here for three years, Hendrix! I spent three years with people who were planning to kill everybody I loved! And now you show up, right around the time they're caught? It's too much of a coincidence." Alia sniffles, and wipes tears from her red eyes. "I can't trust you. I just can't."

She sprints away, her feet imprinting marks in the snow. I want to follow; I long to chase after her and wrap her in my arms and gain her trust again. I want her to believe in me. She is my safe place. I want to look into those beautiful green eyes framed with those thick lashes. I want to touch her cheeks, rosy from the crisp air. I want to take her hair, her hair which reminds me so much of Rapunzel, and I want to climb it. I want to save her, the damsel in distress. I want to unlock her from her tower, and unleash the true Alia.

And suddenly I know it. I've fallen in love.

It's crazy; I never thought it would happen. After growing up with an abusive father and a mother who doesn't know how to stand up for herself, I vowed to never get married. I was raised thinking relationships just end up bringing pain to someone you love. I guess meeting Alia Wordsworth changed all that.

But I don't chase after her, and I don't wrap her in my arms and gain her trust and her belief. I don't save her, the damsel in distress. Instead I follow a separate trail; one I know won't lead me back to her.

"Two roads diverged in a wood and I—I took the one less travelled by, and that has made all the difference."

***

Robert Frost.

Possibly the only person who has ever saved me from situations I feel utterly hopeless in; which is why I flip to the very back of my book, where I have scrawled the words of famous poets who deserve more credit than they have gotten.

I remember sitting at my desk in the fourth grade, before society wasn't really all that different. There were no genetically modified humans, to say the least. We still had textbooks, that I know. My teacher, Mrs. Sheets, had told us to turn to page 401. After that, I was hooked.

Here's the thing about Frost: he understands people. Most people struggle to understand their fellow men, but Robert Frost could. Take some of his most renowned works, for example. "Nothing Gold Can Stay" revealed the tragedies change can cause, and how you should cherish what you have before it's gone. But that day in class, we read "The Road Not Taken," and it was life-changing. How much he understood the hardships of deciding, and the aftermath of each decision you make throughout your existence, it was just incredible. After reading that poem, I knew that was what I wanted to do. I wanted to inspire people with my words.

I received my book in fourth grade, after I came home and told Mom that I wanted to be a writer. She smiled this amazing smile, something she almost never did. She gave me this book she'd had hidden away in the attic. *This belonged to someone very close to you,* she had said. *Don't lose it.* I remember opening it and seeing 'Mary Asher' scribbled on the leathery inside cover, but I didn't think much of it. Not until now.

The pages were yellowed even then, but they were all blank except for the first two. On the first one there was this poem, "The Improbability of You and I." I'm not for sure, but I think it was written about my dad after she got the news he died in war.

They say that bumblebees

Aren't supposed to fly,

But they also say

I wasn't meant to

Step foot through the gate

Of your white picket fence.

It was the first time I saw

The crystals in your eyes,

And little did I know that

We would soon say our goodbyes.

Then the summer ran away

And the sun set to its grave and I thought

Perhaps we must wait

For the dead of winter

To shed off our skin

So we can blossom

Like the daffodils I saw

In your mom's backyard.

And yet there still will

Come a day when I

Take the pieces of you

Off the top shelf in my closet

And try to fit the lost

Memories together like a

Broken jigsaw puzzle.

But they don't align

Like they

Used

To.

On that last page was written in messy cursive, "Two roads diverged in a wood and I—I took the one less travelled by, and that has made all the difference." I didn't think much of that either, at the time, but I sure do now. My mother did take the road less travelled by, and it did make a difference; I'm just not sure if it's good or bad. That was Frost's intention though. And honestly, he's right.

I have written other quotes from other famous poets in the book, but that one will always be my favorite. And when I read it now, I don't know what to think. Robert Frost's words can usually help me through any situation, but this time I don't know if they can.

"Hey," It's Reed. I shove my book in my pocket, stand up, and walk over to him.

"Hey." Reed was a close friend of Vinny's. He must be devastated.

"So I guess you're manning the fort while they're in prison, huh?" he questions, in reference to Cleo and Vinny's campground. "You have any idea when they're comin' back out?" I stare into his eyes and notice they're watery, and have formed purple bags underneath them.

"Uh, they're not coming back out, Reed. They're going to be killed."

His jaw clenches. "You tellin' me they gonna be shot? You messin' with me, boy? You think this is funny?" Waves of anger are radiating off of him.

"I'm sorry, Reed."

He collapses on the ground. "I can't believe this. Those damn bastards are leavin' me."

Reed's not someone you would believe to be sensitive. He's got this rough look to him, a bunch of scars on his face and tattoos snaking up his biceps. When he starts to cry, I don't know how to react.

"Are you okay?"

He snorts. "Peachy. Just love it when my best friends stab me in the back and run off gettin' killed." He stands up, brushing off his pants. "I still love em' though. I'll always love my Cleo and Vinny." He gives me one last glance, then walks away.

I spend the rest of the day roasting an excess number of marshmallows over the fire. I would kill something, but I don't know how to cook an animal correctly, and I'd prefer not getting food poisoning. Eventually, I get sick of it, and decide to head down to The Lot.

The feeling in the air is weird. It's like half The Lot is mourning over the loss of their beloved friends, and the other half is ready to throw their traitors into the depths of Hell.

Without even looking, I know which group Alia is in.

I wander over to the mob of angry protesters. It's like they've morphed into these gothic creatures overnight. A majority of the people are wearing all black, but covered with chains and skulls, the women donning dark lipstick and heavy eyeliner. Some have black and red streaks running through their hair. I spot Alia right away, however. Her bright blonde hair sticks out amongst the black, and her dress is navy.

"Hey, Alia."

She swivels around. "Oh, it's you. Hey everyone! I've found the traitors' secret weapon!"

Fifty pairs of shadowy eyes meet mine. I hear a lot of sentences hollered, but wouldn't dare repeat due to the amount of foul language.

A short, chubby man steps forward. "This place is for The Awakened only! We know you're a part of The Forces, give up the act! I'm not afraid to shoot!" He may be short, but he does have a gun. I back away slowly.

"This ends now." I grab one of the protester's megaphones and yell as loud as I can:

"Everyone! My name is Hendrix Asher. I know none of you are too fond of me right now. Hell, I'm not even fond of me. But I will say this; I had no part in Cleo and Vinny's plot against all of you. I didn't even know any of you until yesterday. I knew nothing about The Awakened or The Forces or how we're doomed and everything. But I'm with you! I am a part of The Awakened, and I'm going to embrace it! So, here's what I say. I know you all feel like you've been given some sort of burden by being a part of this, but society is counting on us to stop The Forces from causing further destruction. I know it's terrifying; I'm scared shitless right now. But we've got to quit hiding away! So hear me out; what if we left? What if we left this hideout, went to the president, and told him we're here to serve? Guys, we were given a purpose. Our purpose is this. And our purpose is now. I don't care if you like it or not, but it's the truth. So, what do you say?"

Applause erupts from everywhere.

***

The president glares at the fragile man. He is weak and trembling, but the president doesn't care.

He needs answers.

In suit and tie, he sits across from the man. The man is handcuffed at the wrists and ankles, with three guns pressed against the back of his head; as if he'd dare to make a move.

"State your name."

The man whimpers.

"State your name!"

"Mudabbir!"

Mudabbir knows little English. It is easy to tell, for his eyes are glossy and opaque when he is addressed.

"Mudabbir, are you associated with The Forces?"

He is silent; then he nods.

"I would like you to explain to me exactly how you are involved with their members."

Mudabbir nods again. He begins to speak his own language, Javanese, which is then translated to English. The translator speaks while he is talking.

"I found out about it because one of their leaders is my uncle. My parents died while I was young, so I always looked up to him. He convinced me to join. I've never killed anyone, but I am the messenger."

"What is the duty of the messenger?"

Mudabbir is confused by the president's words, until the translator repeats it. "The leaders, they have learned about your secret weapons. The people with the special genetics that you will use to battle against them. It was my job to come here several months before The Forces and spy on your people. Then they are able to plan a strategy and defeat your country. We also have some Americans helping us, and in return they get high amounts of currency."

"When are they coming?"

He is silent, until the president speaks again. "If you do not answer right now, you will be forced to."

Mudabbir gulps. "Exactly one month and seven days."

"I see." The president's face creases with worry, and he struggles to remain calm. "Who are they, and why are they here?"

"Indonesia is not going to live!" Mudabbir has tears creeping down his face, and his breathing is rapid. "Ever since we have entered the year of 2030, everybody is fighting, the government is corrupted... somebody needed to take some control." His voice dropped to a whisper. "The world looks down on our people. We have decided it is time to fight for authority, and by tearing every country to ruins, we will have done just that."

"How many have you successfully killed?"

"Approximately 300 million."

The president's face turns stark. He stands up and faces his guards.

"It is time to pursue our advancements." He begins to tremble. "Gather them now. It is time they Awaken."

———

"How many people are there?" I turn towards Alia.

"About five thousand, but that's just an assumption. The Awakened are scattered all over the nation. We have more or less 200 here right now, and I'm betting about 2,500 have already been Placed. The rest are out there somewhere."

"Do they know what they are?"

Alia shakes her head. "Some probably know that they're a part of this, but not all. Listen, I remembered something. You're in a state of quintessence, which means you can transfer between here and your actual body at any given moment. I know for a fact that there are several patients currently in that hospital with you, who are a part of The Awakened."

I'm bewildered. "How could you possibly know that?"

"We all have a sort of magnetism towards each other, which you'll realize eventually. I need you to get those patients out of that hospital, though. It's important we have as many people as possible if we're going to get through this war."

I nod in agreement. "Okay. What if my body isn't healed though?"

"Hey," she steps closer towards me and hugs me. "I know you can do this. You know you can do this."

I hug her back. "Thank you. Where should I meet you after?"

"Back here, and go as fast as you can."

"Got it."

"Okay," she kisses me on the cheek. "Good luck, Hendrix."

I have the urge to kiss her back, but I refrain. "I'll see you in a bit."

Then the cold hits me like a blast.

I open my eyes and inhale deeply, and glance around at the sterile hospital environment. No doctors around. I examine my body. Considering it endured an explosion, it doesn't look that bad.

But it hurts like hell. My joints ache like crazy, but I force them to move. It feels like I haven't used my body in forever. It's a very weird sensation, as if I'm learning to walk again.

I observe the hospital for any possible closets, and finally find one. It's filled with spare doctor uniforms. I slip on a lab coat and hook a stethoscope around my neck. For now, my nametag announces that I am Robert, casual doctor raising no suspicions.

I begin to wander through the hospital, nobody genuinely noticing my presence. I hear a lot of crying and wailing from a hallway, and peer around a corner to see what all the fuss is about.

A corpse is lying in the center of a hallway, pale skin getting paler by the second, and blinding platinum hair to match. Blood is gushing from her head. I gag at the sight.

But somehow I feel drawn to her.

Wait; this is it! This must be what Alia was describing, when you are in the presence with one who is Awakened, you feel drawn to them.

However, she is not awake. She is dead.

Or so I thought until her eyes shoot open and blood spews from her mouth.

Nurses begin pounding at her chest, struggling to get air pumping through her lungs. She shakes violently, as if she's having a seizure. I feel bad for her. She would've been better off dead, instead of living her last moments like this.

"C'mon, Platinum!" A man with dark hair and green eyes collapses on the floor beside her, and clasps his hands while reciting a prayer.

Platinum. The name dances in my head, as if I am somehow familiar with it.

"Platinum!" I yell. She somehow manages to twist her head and meet my gaze. And in that gaze we communicate something, though I'm not exactly sure what it is. I'll see her again, though. I'll see her soon.

I continue my hunt through the building, knowing I have to do it fast. Alia will freak out if I don't make it back to her quickly enough.

Then I see a girl. She has bright red hair and the greenest eyes I've ever seen. I'm drawn to her as well, and I know right then and there that she must mean something.

Before I leap into action, I spot a secretary's desk nearby, but no secretary. Quickly, I rummage through the desk doors. Aha, duct tape! Mustering up my strength, I sprint towards her and she screams, but I muffle her voice with a piece of the duct tape. Frantically searching for something to hide the girl in, I spot a closet labeled "Mortuary Supplies." After flinging open the door and snatching what appears to be a body bag, I carefully zip it open and shove her inside.

"I'll explain later," I whisper before zipping the girl up. I feel awful, but I'm planning on releasing her once we get outside. I hoist her over my shoulder, and make a run towards the hospital doors. I need to get back to Alia.

I am stopped in my tracks.

"Where do you think you're going?"

Part 4

Alia

The time is coming close.

I can feel it in my bones, the adrenaline soaring through my veins like fighter jets. I've been training for this all my life, and finally the moment is here.

Finally.

I was seven years old when it happened. I can vividly remember sleeping soundly in my bedroom, until the front door made the same screech it always does when it's used. Dad never fixed it, always claiming to be too occupied with other things to worry about such a minor thing. The screech echoed through the house more than usual this time, though. I jumped out from under the floral covers, my curious young brain commanding me to investigate.

They were all downstairs, lined up in a row. I remember my slippers, stepping down the old staircase ever so softly, though I was afraid the kitchen light would bounce off their sequins and catch the attention of my mother. She was sitting at the dining room table; if you could even call it that. It was more of a wooden stump surrounded by wooden chairs that callused the fingers I would consistently rub on them. I was an unruly little girl, with a need to constantly be doing something. I still have the attention span of a small child; I can't seem to grow out of it. Maybe it'll come in handy someday.

I specifically remember that my mother was crying. Up until then, I had always thought adults just didn't cry. They were mature and strong. But there was my mother, tears streaming down her face, and I couldn't stop myself from wanting to help her. I was too kind of a person back then, my mind still possessing its child-like innocence and purity. I ran by her side, nuzzling my face in her shoulder. She pulled away, stunned. "Alia? What are you doing up, darling?"

She stroked my blonde locks with her fingers, as if there weren't soldiers lining the room. "Mommy, what are those men doing here?" I had managed to squeak out.

She cupped my face with her palms.

"These men are—"

"The girl!" one of them yelled. "Is she your child?"

My mother wrapped her arms around me. "Yes, and she has nothing to do with you. She is not involved with this."

Another of the men raised his gun. "We want the girl."

My father suddenly barged into the kitchen, donning an army green uniform and clenching a rifle. "We do not accept your offer, Ubayy. I suggest you leave our property now, or I will be forced to take desperate measures."

"Fine. We will leave your home. Thank you for your time, Mr. Wordsworth." They filed out one by one, marching in a perfectly straight line.

I thought I would never see the men again. It was all a haze, really. My parents assured me there was nothing to fret about, go back to bed. All would be well come morning. I huddled into my covers, safe and sound—until that sharp screech from the sliding of my large bedroom window. I awoke, startled, but then a flashlight blinded me. I really did try to scream, make any sound, really, but a cloth was shoved down my throat before I could do anything.

The rest of the night was a blur. Shouting. Darkness. Blood. Gun shots. It was the most horrifying night of my life. It was also the night that changed my life forever.

Flash-forward nine years, post-kidnapping. My mentor, who goes by the name of Mudabbir, has finished my training just in time. We've been preparing for this our entire lives. I don't really remember much of my early youth, so everyone who raised me here, at The Hideout, has had a bigger imprint on me than my biological parents ever had; my only clear memory of them was that last time I saw them.

We are The Forces. The country of Indonesia is corrupted. The inhabitants in this part of the world, near Brunei and Singapore, are terribly undermined for their beliefs and ways of life. I was recruited at a young age to be a part of their U.S. branch in West Lake, New York, and fight alongside their secret rebellion.

I have been taught to believe that the United States government is a throne of lies. That the country I was born in is the real enemy. And in some ways, I agree. Their ways of persuasion and manipulation are quite forceful.

But there are other days when I just stare in the mirror, and I see something different. I say I am a warrior and I say I am a fighter; that I am filled with the same anger and utter hatred that The Forces are. Sometimes, though, my thoughts don't match what I say or do. I gaze in that mirror for a second too long, and see a typical teenage girl. She attends a normal high school, has a normal group of friends, and she's happy. She's gorgeous, with luscious blonde hair and clean skin and big green eyes. Completely different from the girl who gets scolded when she smiles, is prohibited from making contact with other people outside her clan, and has greasy blonde hair that hasn't been washed in three days. The eyes are what saddens me most, however. Not a hint of light in them, no matter how deep I look.

It is this that has me thinking. Would it be so bad to leave? What if I don't want to be the bad guy, sometimes? What if sometimes I wish—no, I long for the opportunity to be rid of it all. How different would it be if I wasn't kidnapped that one night?

But then I get out of my head, because there's no point in dreaming if you're living a nightmare day after day.

***

It's my turn to be called in. It's got to be.

We had our testing yesterday. It takes a grueling amount of time to prepare for, and the testing itself is absolutely arduous. Between the time one turns fifteen and sixteen, you spend forty hours each week training for this; scoring day. The training consists of primarily fighting, though we are also trained in areas like decoding computers and hacking into complex systems. It is vital to be a six or above, or otherwise you are deemed worthless. I can't even begin to explain what happens to those poor souls. If you are a five, you'll get assigned janitorial duty; picking up stray arrows after target practice, wiping the blood off the fighting mats, etc. If you are a one, you become a target for shooting practice. You die.

I had to shoot a one once while practicing my aim. Her name was Lis. I really liked Lis. Sure, she wasn't very coordinated or strong; she was kidnapped like me, but never embraced her newfound home as I have. Then again, she was taken at thirteen, and I was taken at seven, so she wasn't raised here like I was. Lis was always really shy and quiet, and scared to death of everything. But she was so sweet, and cared so much for those around her. Shooting her was the hardest thing I've ever had to do. Mudabbir was screaming at me after I refused, "You are not going to improve if you do not listen! Now shoot! Shoot her in the head!" I couldn't even watch the bullet pierce her brain, and was already sobbing by the time her lifeless body hit the ground.

"Alia Wordsworth, enter room three for scoring."

Please don't let me be a one.

Once I enter the room, the steel door slams behind me. An official-looking woman is sitting at a desk, and beckons me to sit across from her.

"Wordsworth, Alia?" I nod in response. "Please look at the screen behind me for your score."

A screen drops down from the ceiling. Suddenly, my face appears in the center of it.

"Alia Wordsworth." A monotone female voice says from the speakers. "Eight."

A flashing number eight pops up above my head. Then the projection stops.

I can't believe it.

"Congratulations, Alia."

I can't contain my excitement. I jump up and give the woman a hug. "I'm an eight!"

She laughs. "Yes, that's a very good score, especially for a female. You should be proud."

And I am. I am so unbelievably proud and grateful for my score. The average score for a woman is a seven. I am special.

Mudabbir is waiting for me when I exit the scoring room. So many times, I have seen people walk out of this room with tears running down their face. Sometimes, their mentor will be waiting for them. They will slap them in the face, scolding their foolish score. But it's worse when there's no one waiting for you at all. It's worse when your mentor is so disappointed in you that they don't even bother to show up.

I'm so glad I'm not one of those people. Instead, Mudabbir has this enormous grin plastered on his face, the kind that goes all the way up to his eyes. I run into his arms, and he twirls me in a circle.

"I am so very proud." He's been like a father to me. It means the world to hear him praise me like that.

"Thank you."

He nods. "Of course. You do know the meaning of your score, correct?"

I shake my head. "Well, it means that I can do basically whatever job I want, right?"

"No, Alia." He doesn't meet my gaze. "You have to go Outside."

"What? No, that cannot be true." I stammer, trying to ponder his words. "I can't—"

"Come with me."

I follow him through the glass doors.

We sit down in one of the private conference rooms. "Men and women who are scored with an eight or above are automatically assigned to be Outside guardians. It has been confirmed that the American president has a way to fight back against us and win. Those who have a score such as your own must foil his plan."

"What is his plan, exactly?"

He swallows. "They have these people called The Awakened. Ultimate modified soldiers who can battle any demon with limitless strength and immunity. It is your duty to find these people, socialize with them, and eventually figure out a way to outsmart them."

"That's crazy! There's no way in hell I'm doing that!" I stand up and rush out of the room.

"You don't have a choice!"

When have I ever had a choice? It dawns on me that I'd rather be a five than an eight any day. At least I wouldn't be forced to risk my life.

———

Later that evening, I slip into my bath robe and crawl into bed. The other girls do the same. I absolutely hate the sleeping quarters. Imagine sleeping in a warehouse with metallic cots and bright fluorescent lighting that won't be shut off until all two hundred and twelve girls are completely ready for bed. It sucks.

The sleeping situation is primarily worst, though, when the nightmares come. Though the kidnapping was years ago, there are times in the night when images flash through my mind, too terrifying to describe. I can still recall the feeling of the cloth down my throat, and sometimes amid my slumber a scream leaps from my lungs. Not only does it awaken the other girls, but I receive a cruel beating from Ubayy.

Speak of the devil. "Where is Cleodora?" Ubayy stands at the front of the room. I didn't even see him walk in.

I glance over at the bed next to mine, and sure enough, Cleo's missing. She's probably off sleeping with some guy again.

"Did you ask Vin?" someone shouts. I actually really like Vinny. Even though he's Cleo's twin, he's completely the opposite of her. Sure, he drinks a beer every once in a while, but besides that, he's very down to earth.

"Yes, he does not know of her location."

Reed, Vinny's best friend, bursts through the door, shoving Ubayy out of his way.

"Is anybody in here an Eight or above?"

All the girls shake their heads. Well, all except me.

"Alia?" he summons me over. "Come with me."

I hurriedly try to keep up with his pace. Beads of sweat trickle off his forehead, and his hands tremor. "Reed, what's going on?"

"Cleo!" his voice is shaking. "She ran Outside."

"Are you serious?" If he is, this is awful.

"Yes! I don't know how she got out, but she did. You're the only one eligible. I need you to stop her."

"I can't!"

"You *can*." His jaw clenches.

"I'll give you fifteen minutes to gather whatever belongings you need. Be back by tomorrow's sunset."

"What if I don't want to?" I back away. "What if I refuse to do this?"

With a stark white face and eyes ablaze, he says those dreaded words, words that have become a fiend to my own perspective.

"You don't have a choice."

***

Sixteen hours and counting.

That's how long I've been awake, keeping my eyes pried open and searching within the Ferncliff Forest for any sign of Cleo. This entire situation is a mess.

I cannot help wondering why she did it. Why anyone would even consider going Outside, I have no idea. We've been told that the people out here have no morals. They're just wild, greedy animals, who put themselves before anyone else. Anyone who is led by a democratic government is wicked, and therefore should be punished. At least, that's what we've been taught. It's what I've had drilled into my head time and time again: "Everyone outside of The Forces is evil, and they need to be set straight."

"Going somewhere?"

My heart leaps, and I spin around to face the source of the deep voice.

"Ezra Callahan." He walks up close to me and shakes my hand.

"Alia Wordsworth." His blue eyes seem to pierce mine in a brazen manner.

"What are you doing out in the middle of the woods, Alia?"

"I could ask you the same question. Or do you just have a hobby of spying on strange women in unexpected places?" I glare at him.

"Touché." He has dark brown hair and a five o'clock shadow, donning a clearly worn flannel.

"Seriously, what are you doing out here? I'm sorry, but it doesn't seem likely to run into a stranger in the middle of the woods without a good explanation."

"You wouldn't understand it. I don't even understand why I'm out here, if I'm being completely honest."

I raise my eyebrows. "Try me."

Ezra clears his throat. "Uh, okay, but you'll be questioning my sanity after I tell you this." A nervous laugh erupts from his throat. "I'm part of The Awakened. Just found out a few days ago, actually. One of my buddies told me to find his campground in this area, but he didn't give me an exact location, so now I'm kinda doomed. You?" He smirks.

A red light goes off in my head. This is my chance to interact with the enemy. Fate has given me the opportunity to do my job; I may as well do it right. "Actually, I'm in the same situation as you."

He grins. "Seriously? Well, that's coincidental. I guess it makes sense, though, considering you don't seem like the type of person who enjoys hunting in the middle of November."

After only a few minutes of observing his actions, I can already tell one thing; he uses humor as a defense mechanism. I wonder if this applies to all who are The Awakened.

"Kinda sucks when both your parents are dead and you wake up one day and realize your entire life's been a lie, doesn't it?"

"Oh my god, I'm so sorry!"

He shakes his head. "I'm sorry for you too."

Oh, right.

"Yeah, it's hard." I sit down and lean back against a nearby tree. "Care to join me?"

Ezra sits beside me. "Don't mind if I do."

I look into his eyes. "So, tell me about how it all went down. You know, with the whole Awakened thing."

His face turns hard and stone-like, and he breaks our gaze. "Last Monday at about 3:00 a.m., my friend Sage burst into my house through my bedroom window. I'm still not sure how he got up there, because my bedroom's on the top level. Anyway, some of the glass he broke from the window pierced my eyelid, so of course I woke up and started screaming my head off because I'm not used to people coming through my window in the middle of the night and stabbing my eye out. He whispered to me, 'They're coming, we have to leave now.' So with my eye oozing blood and temporarily blinded, I followed him out of the house without even notifying my parents. Stupid decision, I curse myself for it every second. He explained that I'm a part of this whole mess, and that we needed to escape, and escape fast. You know, with the whole charade about the government beginning the Placement and that if they find us we're done for. I mean, I always thought I was a little different than anyone else…kind of an outcast in school, but nothing like this. It's all kinda surreal right now. What about you?"

Crap. I need to make something up. "Same thing, besides the whole temporary blindness thing. I just don't understand why these Forces could be so evil as to wanting to tear apart our nation of freedom, when we didn't even do anything to provoke them."

And suddenly I'm no longer pretending, but speaking straight from my heart. I'm the evil one. Not the Americans, not any other country in existence; me. I've been on the wrong side this entire time, and I better set my alliances straight before someone gets hurt. Correction; before the rest of the world gets hurt by people who have no idea of the true pain they're putting these innocent people through. Something needs to be done, and the only person who has the capability of doing that is myself.

146

Ezra sets his hand on my thigh. A risky move. "Exactly." He stands up, brushing the stray dirt from his pants. Then, he reaches out his hand. "Care to join me?"

I nod, linking my cold fingers through his warm ones. "Don't mind if I do."

***

I don't notice when the gun goes off.

It's kind of like that one time when I was seven, after the kidnapping, and Mudabbir let me go outside in the courtyard. I was with my best friend at the time, though I can't even recall her name now. Something with a J, I think. We'd been running along the path with these boats we'd made out of tinfoil from our leftover lunch packs (we were never allowed to have real toys). It had been raining really hard that day, so we set the boats along the small river of water flowing beside the curb. We ran and ran, trying to keep our pace with them. I was having so much fun; I didn't even notice the bullet when it hit my side. I just kept smiling through it all. My friend knew, though. I remember her face going white and her jaw going slack and her scream that was louder than any gunshot. She screeched "Red!" but I thought she said "Run!" so I laughed harder and ran faster. I didn't even feel the blood dripping down my leg, hot and seething. I didn't feel the slightest bit of pain.

Flash-forward ten years. A gunshot sounds in the distance, but we don't think much of it. Probably a hunter searching for game.

It's Ezra who first notices. "Hey, are you okay?"

147

I realize my hand is pressed to my side, and red smears start appearing from the spaces between my knuckles. When I remove it, blood gushes from just below my ribcage.

"Oh my god, why didn't you say anything? I didn't know that bullet hit you!"

I shake my head. "It doesn't hurt."

Ezra opens his mouth, then thinks better of himself and shuts it. "Right. I forgot."

"What?"

"We're immune to things like this. We're Awakened."

"Right."

But my stomach doesn't settle. I am not Awakened; I should not be immune to things like this.

"Come on. Let's get that bullet out of your side before an infection sets in."

He buries his hand in the pocket of his jeans and pulls out a first aid kit. It turns out, Ezra is some sort of miracle doctor. I lay there on my side, still numbed, listening to the light drumming of his fingers against my bare skin.

I hear the hissing of a thread, most likely stitching up the wound. "So, are you a certified surgeon or something?"

He laughs a deep and gravelly chuckle. "Or something."

"Do tell."

"Before my dad died, he was a neurosurgeon. He'd lecture me every night on how 'medicine is not just an occupation, it's an art and way of life'. You don't know how many brains I've watched my dad jab needles into."

"So, you're really interested in spending your life 'upholding the art of medicine'?"

His shoulders droop. "It's all I know."

"You don't know your true passion. That's really sad."

A grim look appears on his face. I notice for the first time how hollow his cheeks are and how there's almost no light in his eyes. He looks tired. "My passion is medicine."

"No, it's not. Medicine is your father's passion. You're not your father."

"You don't know me or my family. You're a stranger; you have no place in saying anything."

I stand up as soon as he finishes the last of the stitches. Not even a sting.

"I do know you. You're the kid who was forced into conformity since the minute you were born. You were the kid who was told what he should be and became it. You never actually used your own mind because you were so busy listening to the needs of others. And at night, it would eat you alive, feeling trapped in your own skin while trying to fit the standards of what society wants-"

"*Stop!* Just *stop.*" The shadows on his face seems to have darkened.

"Look. I don't know you, okay? But you seem to know me pretty damn well. So I'm going to say this. My life hasn't been great. I followed in the footsteps of my parents. That's just how I was raised. But I didn't do it just because of that. I was always really shy, believe it or not, and the kids in school would never talk to me and they'd call me names and whatever. It sucked. But my parents, they were admired by *everyone*. We'd walk down a street, and people I've never even seen in my life would hug my parents and barely give me a second glance. Same with school. I never had anyone, except for Sage, my best friend. Sage didn't go to my school, though, so my status didn't matter to him. Anyway, I thought that if I could grow up and be like my parents, I might be able to fit in for a change. I hate it, but it feels better to be on the inside than the outside."

I can't even breathe. That was raw and remarkable and brilliant. "You are amazing."

"Well, that's better than being called 'Ez the Lez.'"

"'Lez' as in 'lesbian?' That is so bad."

He nods. "Yeah, it was. It was kinda crazy, though. Once everyone figured out how smart I am, they'd be totally nice and friendly just so I could help them with their biology homework."

I shrug. "Yeah. Well, we'd better get going if we want to reach that campground."

We walk in silence for several hours. I stare at the sunset, deliberating whatever fate is planning that would somehow make me run into the unique soul that is Ezra Callahan.

He suddenly stops and turns towards me. "I think that's what I learned throughout everything. About society, I mean."

"What is that?"

His blue eyes meet mine, and I start drowning. "People will stab you in the back, then ask you why you're bleeding."

***

"She liked the winters."

I stop and stare at him for a moment. "How do you know?"

He looks down the path for a moment, trapped in its spooling mystery and overwhelming endlessness that most humans feared, but Ezra seemed to have a liking towards. Maybe the idea of a long journey comforted him. He could hide from the truth longer. "I looked her up, of course. After Sage told me my entire life was constructed of lies, he also told me her name."

"Which was?"

He swallows. "Avril."

"What about your dad?"

"Atticus. He died in war, like all the others. Fighting The Forces."

I nod. "So, winters. Was your mom a snowflake analyzer or something?"

A grin appears on his face, but doesn't spread to his eyes. They're still hard, and cold. "There's this photo of her when I searched her up. She was listed as one of the Embryo Donors, but there was this image next to her name. There was an image next to every woman's name, but hers stood out. All the others had these lackluster photos that resembled a dreary yearbook picture. But in hers, she was standing in the midst of a blizzard and was wrapped in this shimmery blue coat with her arms thrown up in the air like she was catching the snowflakes in her hands. I could tell by her eyes. They looked like snowflakes, grey but with a few sapphire sparkles glinting from the camera flash. Like ice crystals had fallen from the sky and immersed themselves into them." He looks down. "It's hard to explain, I guess."

"Well you explained it beautifully."

Ezra sets one of his abrasive hands upon my shoulder. I shrink back, the energy within him much too intoxicating. He has such a fire in him suddenly, like bringing back memories of his past provokes him in a way that's not really seen as angry, but more vengeful than anything. Sixteen years of his life he didn't even know the woman who gave birth to him.

And now, it's too late.

"What about you? What are your parents like?"

I try to recall the faint memories I have. Faint facial features, small mannerisms, nothing too significant. Then again, nothing ever is the first seven years of life. So instead, I try and imagine them how I'd hoped they were. I'd given the subject a lot of thought.

"My mom looked exactly like me, but ten times prettier. She had this golden blonde hair that looked like Rapunzel's and emeralds for eyes. My dad, however, looked nothing like me. Dark hair, dark eyes, very brooding. They were the sweetest people, though. Always looking out for everyone, including each other. During family game nights, they'd always let me win…" I sigh.

"Yeah." He continues to stare down the winding path ahead of us, and I stare too, trying to see the certain promise he does. "I'm going to be honest with you, I have no idea where we're going."

I laugh along with him. "Neither do I."

Ezra's brows begin to furrow, and he points somewhere ahead of me. "Look."

I squint my eyes only to spot a woman off in the distance near the Hudson River, now a rushing current of water; a woman who vaguely resembles Cleo. The figure leaps onto a small boat and lets the force of the river carry her down.

I shake my head. "We've gotta go."

"What?"

"Just follow me."

He grabs my shoulder. "You sure your clothes are suitable? I don't normally care for fashion, but if we're going to go trekking through the woods for a long period of time…"

I glance down, embarrassed. My attire isn't exactly fit for venturing out into the woods. Reed hadn't even given me time to change, so I'm stuck in a white see-through nightgown (which goes perfect with my black bra) and a pair of raggedy slippers that are one-size too small.

"Hey," Ezra reaches into his backpack and tosses me some torn up sneakers. "These will better suit you than those flimsy slippers you have."

I nod. "Yeah, thanks. Why do you have these?"

He shrugs. "I brought anything I thought could come in handy. I thought an extra pair of shoes couldn't hurt."

"Good idea." We take off in a sprint, jumping over logs and dodging fallen timber. The river's only about a couple hundred yards away, so it only takes about a few minutes to reach it.

"Here, I'll make us a temporary raft. You keep watch and don't lose sight of that girl in front of us."

It takes me several hours to gather the right materials. I have to find logs that are strong enough; this involves my using a skill I learned several years ago in my training. If a log is weak enough that, when kicked, it makes any sort of movement, it is too weak for constructional use. I spend a while kicking logs to find the right ones, and spend more time exploring the forest until I spot vines snaking up a lonesome tree trunk. I tear them off easily, and head back to camp.

Ezra is there when I get back. I notice he saved me a lot of time by already making the oars out of what looks like branches.

"Thank you for making the oars. Glad you're thinking ahead."

"No problem. You need any help putting that together?"

I roll my eyes. "I think I got it."

"Suit yourself." He continues to fiddle with a nearby twig as I spend a laborious two hours crafting the raft in silence.

"Who is she, anyway?" He questions, finally breaking the drawn-out quiet. "That girl who was floating down the river. Or do you have a habit of befriending random strangers in the woods?"

I shake my head. "She's my friend. She ran away a couple days ago."

"Oh, is she also part of the Awakened? Don't really blame her. I wanted to run away myself when I first found out. Just fall off the face of the earth."

"Yeah, I think that's what her train of thought was."

"But she didn't even give you a warning? Damn, some friend she is."

"We weren't that close."

"I'm pretty sure running away into the woods and disappearing from existence isn't only something you share with your closest BFF."

He pulls his shirt off, using the worn, smooth cloth to dab at his face. I don't understand how it's possible for someone to be sweating as much as he is in forty-degree weather, but I push the thought aside. He's quite fit, so I don't exactly mind it.

"Hey, how'd you learn all this stuff? I mean when we were running, you seemed like you knew what we were doing. When I jump I look like a flailing cat, but you look like an Amazon warrior chick. And your construction skills are badass, I might add."

I stand back to admire my handiwork. What was once four separate logs is now a raft woven together with honeysuckle vines and two oars created with chopped off branches.

"When I was a kid, I was kind of a tomboy. I would put myself up to challenges like climbing oak trees and chopping firewood. Building things like boats and rafts with whatever was handy was one of my favorite hobbies." At least I didn't have to lie about this. Even though we had to train most days, when you were under the age of twelve you got at least one free hour in the day for leisure activities.

"Really? I wouldn't peg you as the tomboy type. You seem more like one of the cool girls, with that bright blonde hair and oblivious aura."

I shrug. "I guess there's a lot you don't know about me."

He grins a wide grin, this time reaching all the way up to his eyes. "I guess so."

I gesture towards the boat. "You ready to go?"

He nods. "Always up for a rapid river chase with a badass Amazon warrior."

***

Ezra's strength is put to good use. He lifts up the raft with ease and tosses it into the water. It floats, and the current pulls against the anchor line I staked to the bank.

Ezra gives me a weary gaze. "You sure about this?"

"Positive." I unlatch the vine from its stake in the ground and hand it to him. "Okay, I'll jump on first, then you follow suit. Got it?"

"Roger that." He yanks the raft as close to shore as he can. The water's rough, but I can handle it. My departure from land to log is nothing short of smooth.

"I don't think we'll be able to make much progress tonight. It's getting darker by the minute. We also don't want to risk catching hypothermia with the cold temperature of the water plus the air."

He's right. At night, the temperature is surely going to drop below freezing. The water isn't exactly warm either.

"As long as we steer clear of getting wet, we shouldn't be at risk for illness. Now hurry up, we're losing daylight." I grasp onto the vines to use as a type of handle to keep myself steady atop the raft, and run my fingers along the splintery edges of my oar.

"Okay, okay." Ezra extends his leg out towards me, but the river gains momentum and unexpectedly jerks the raft.

He plunges into the current.

"Ezra!" My heart sinks. The water begins to sweep me away, the agile raft gliding over the rocks upon the surface with ease.

I've lost sight of Ezra. The whitecaps bubbling at the surface make it difficult to spot anything underneath. Tears stream down my face.

"Ezra!" I bury my head in my hands. "Please."

I stare out across at the land, watching the trees fly by like a cassette tape coming to its end. The colors fuse together, streaks of white and black and grey, a canvas of monotones. I finally look up at the sky, watching the fragile flakes float down, showering my hair and clinging to the ends of my eyelashes. Winter. His mom always liked the winter. But she sacrificed that. She sacrificed the chance of ever experiencing another winter, of ever living out a life with so much promise. She gave up all of that so she could let her son live and thrive.

If I let her son die, it would all be for nothing.

I float a good distance downstream. As my eyes focus in the distance, I spot a figure leaping out of the water about 100 yards away from me. Ezra's alive and safely on land! I pick up the oar and wedge it through a fissure between two of the logs. When shoved deep enough, the end of the oar eventually hits rock bottom. It is surprisingly shallow. I drag it across the river's floor as it carries me farther and farther down its path, until finally, I hit something. The raft stops mid-motion. I've found my anchor.

The vines are tied pretty tight. Why did I have to construct this thing so well? It's not going to give if I just use my bare hands, so I clamp my jaw around the tendrils and grind my teeth hard enough for them to snap. I only let loose one log, thankfully. The rest remain intact while I position the free log in front of me.

"Here goes nothing, Alia." I slip off the raft, the frigid water creeping up my bones instantly. If I stay in here too long, I could potentially get hypothermia and risk death. I take my feet and push off the raft with the loose log angling towards the edge of the river.

As I climb out of the water and struggle to grasp the surface of the land, I realize just how steep it truly is. The land just outside the river is a towering hill, littered with so many rocks the grass is barely visible.

I finally grasp a firm rock and hoist myself up, flinging my body out of the freezing current and onto the rocky surface. I manage to get ahold of my balance, but not for long. The land is too steep for me to walk flat-footed. It would work best if instead I used the tall hill as a rock wall, and climbed in the direction of Ezra.

Just a few minutes into climbing, I misstep onto a rock with an unusually jagged edge. "Shit!" A shooting pain spirals up my leg. It feels like someone just put a knife through my foot. The rocks around me slowly become coated with blood. I can't continue to walk on rocks with an open wound.

I want to gag at the sight of my foot. The cut is deep, dark blood gushing from the torn skin. Remnants of rock are also wedged into the skin, and I can see a small part of my navicular bone.

I do what I have to do, which is tear off a part of my nightgown. The white fabric is horrible quality, so I rip off a long strand and wrap it several times around the wound. It still feels like hell, but at least it's no longer exposed.

"Alia!"

Ezra's voice! My heart leaps and a sense of relief rushes through my veins. "Ezra!"

He's perched safely on land, and I notice how the surface has flattened up ahead. His hair and clothing are drenched and he has a scratch on his face, but other than that he appears to be okay.

"Thank God! I've been searching for you."

He laughs. "Let me help you up." I'm about to decline his offer, when he interrupts me. "It's okay. I've been sitting here for the last twenty minutes, I have enough strength." He lifts me down from the rocks with little effort, but not without noticing my foot. "Oh my god, are you okay? What happened?"

"I'll explain later." I say, my energy too drained to speak.

He nods. "Got it. I know where to get you properly taken care of, though."

Ezra walks in silence for the next thirty minutes, while I lay resting in his arms. I'm glad he doesn't question me. I'm freezing and exhausted to a point where I don't even care to look at where we're going.

After what seems like several miles from where we'd originally started by the river, he stops walking. "Alia, we're here. Open your eyes."

And when I do, I swear I'm dreaming.

"Cleo."

***

The first time I saw Cleo, I was struck into this state of pure wonder. Right away, I felt a dire need to prove my worth to her, like her opinion of me mattered.

And maybe it did. Maybe it's because the primary moment I laid my eyes on her, even as mere first graders, she mesmerized me. Cleo always had that quality to her, the quality that drew people towards her like opposite charged magnets clinging to each other.

I remember like it was yesterday. Cleo was sitting at the Butterfly table, or otherwise known as the table for the smart kids who were kidnapped. I had reluctantly made my way over towards her, staring down at my Mary Jane shoes as I did so. How was I deemed good enough to approach this girl who was nothing less than *It*? Her Mary Janes were clearly new and top of

161

the line, whereas mine were passed down through generations of cousins and scuffed up to the point where they hardly even resembled shoes. Mom had tried to polish them, but they were beyond repair. Her dress was the one I had seen in the window of Macy's, the dress I had begged and sobbed over for ages. I had actually offered to sell my pet fish, Mr. McFins, so I could earn money to buy the dress myself. It was so beautiful to my innocent mind, with its green and blue plaid pattern, finished off with a pink satin bow tied around the waist. It doesn't sound like much, but it was everything to me.

So when Cleo came to school in the dress of my dreams, with her shiny caramel curls cascading down her back and wide green eyes that made anyone who gazed into them melt, I felt inferior. After all, she was 4'4 at the age of seven, where I was 3'11 on a good day. She was different, she was captivating, she was unique... she was special. I could tell that she was someone who was going to go somewhere in life, and she was going to make the most of it.

I was a little girl with big blue eyes and stick-straight hair and a plain black pencil skirt with less-than average shoes. I was nobody.

That's what I realized when Ezra woke me up, and found myself swimming in Cleo's eyes.

I haven't changed. And I never will, unless I make it happen.

Ezra puts his hand on top of mine. I sit up, the cot I'm lying on much too uncomfortable. "We got your foot fixed up. You'll be on crutches for a few days, but Cleo gave you some medicine that will heal your wound extra fast."

I muster a pathetic smile. "Thanks, guys." Cleo's standing in the doorway of the small hut I appear to have fallen asleep in, and I nod in her direction.

My brain is foggy. I don't remember much of the events leading up to now. I do, however, have a thirst clawing at my throat that I need to quench immediately.

"Can you show me where I can find some water?"

Cleo points behind her. "The Springwater pond is a bit of a walk that way. I can come with you and give you some support if you feel unstable on your feet."

I test out my balance to clarify. "Nope, I'm all good." Glancing down, I realize I'm in a grey hoodie and a loose pair of jeans. "Where'd my nightgown go?"

She shrugs. "It was pretty grimy, so I washed it in the Springwater pond and hung it out to dry. Figured you could use some new clothes."

"That was nice of you, thanks. But who changed—"

She laughs. "Don't worry, I took care of you. By the way, does the bra you're wearing fit okay? It's mine, but we're about the same chest size."

I nod. "Yeah, it's okay. I'm going to go get some water."

Ezra's sneakers he lent me are sitting by the doorway, surprisingly dry. Cleo took care of every little thing.

The scene outside is not what I was expecting. I thought Ezra and Cleo had built the hut I was staying in from scratch, or found it and chose to inhabit it; but as soon as I step outdoors, I see that's not the case at all.

There's this whole community of people gathered in a lot of some sort. Teens and adults, all around the same age, laughing and conversing with one another. The lot is surrounded by dozens of trees, and I come to the conclusion that we're hidden in a forest of some sort.

I'm about to go ask Cleo where we're at for affirmation, when a strange man walks up to me. "Hey, you're that chick who's been in the infirmary for the last two days."

Two days? Oh, God. "Uh, yeah, that's me."

The guy is clearly high, or drunk or both. Maybe a little hungover as well. "Damn, woman, how many kegs did you drink?"

I scoff. Kegs? Seriously? "I don't drink."

His eyes zero in on my chest, which I intently cross my arms over.

"Why were you in the infirmary for two days? Oh man, were you like so stoned that you just passed out?"

I swat at his arm. "Go away, asshole."

I keep my head low the rest of my walk to the pond. My stealth mode is successful, until someone taps me on the shoulder from behind.

Ezra.

"Are you okay?"

The one question I absolutely resent right now. "I'm great! Are you kidding? I love the fact that I have no idea where I am or that some guy just asked me if I was stoned. Lovely!"

Ezra puts his hands on my shoulders. "Hey. Calm down. This isn't like you."

I sit down, running my hands through my hair. It's so greasy. Forty-eight hours really does take a toll on your hair.

"Well maybe it's time I changed."

Ezra sits down next to me, and we stare at our reflections in the pond. "What is this about, Alia?"

Inhale. Exhale. "All my life, I've been nobody. I've just done what I've told, becoming what others want me to be. But what if I don't want that anymore?"

Ezra takes my hand and holds it to his chest. "Look, I don't know what brought this on, but you don't need to change for anyone."

"But what if I just realized that I've been blind for my entire life, and for the first time I can see? I can see everything now. I see who I am, and I don't like it."

"Who are you, Alia?"

"I am Awakened."

And for the first time in my life, I know what I just said is nothing less than true.

***

"I have to tell you something."

He nods. "Of course. Anything"

"What I told you before was a lie."

Ezra's eyes widen, blue crystals carved with cracks. "What are you talking about, Alia?"

I look down, avoiding his piercing gaze. "I'm not a part of The Awakened. I'm actually a part of the people trying to destroy your homeland."

His jaw clenches suddenly, and he stumbles as he stands and tries to balance on his own two feet. "You're kidding."

I shake my head. "No, I'm not. But I swear, I've never felt like I'd belonged on their side. Your country is beautiful; I could never be so cruel as to harm it. I'm completely supportive of you."

Ezra's hands run through his thick curls. The spot above his forehead gleams with sweat. "No, I don't want any of your bullshit. You were trying to get information from me so a few weeks later you could come back and shoot me in the head with one of your fancy machine guns."

Tears spill from my eyes. He has it all wrong! "There has to be something I can do to make you believe me. Please, just hear me out."

His eyes, once soft and pure, turn to stone. "I can't."

As he walks away, I begin to count the seconds until he tells everyone my true identity.

It's ironic; an identity is supposed to be a representation of who you are. But in my case, that couldn't be further from the truth.

When I arrive back from the pond, I see Cleo and Ezra conversing, but I'm guessing it's not about me. Cleo's smiling and giggling, her right hand lightly brushing up against Ezra's arm. I could out her, say that she's here for the same reason I am, but I decide not to. Just because I feel awful doesn't mean she has to.

"Hey,"

Someone taps on my shoulder and I spin around. It's a girl, with hair as orange as the pumpkins I used to grow in the courtyard garden.

"Are you new here?"

The words don't want to come out of my mouth, until they finally do, slowly seeping out. "Uh, yeah. Alia Wordsworth."

She sticks her hand out to shake. "Bea."

Bea's fingernails are coated with dirt and grime, but I reluctantly shake her hand anyway. "Hi."

"So, do you already have a campground set up?"

Oh, yeah. That might be a bit useful. "No, not yet."

"Want me to help?"

"Sure. Thanks."

She nods. "No problem, newbie."

I follow Bea to her own campground, where she pulls out a small cardboard box that looks like it hasn't seen the light of day in ages. "What's in there?"

Her long braids smack me in the face when she turns to look at me. "I always keep a spare tent on me in case this one gets destroyed. The spare isn't great quality, but it'll get you by until we move."

"What do you mean, move?"

"We're nomadic; we stay in one place until the government determines our location; then we move into another spot you can barely locate on the map." She grins.

"How often do you move, usually?"

"About every six months. I've been with this group for six years, and that's usually the interval."

I shake my head. "There's more than just one group of the Awakened hiding out?"

Bea looks shocked. It surprises me, though. I never thought of just how many people had been given this burden. And I'm part of the reason why.

"There's dozens of groups. We're a rebellion."

I like the sound of that. A rebellion.

But I have to commit one hundred percent if I'm going to be a part of it. Do I really want to walk away from the only life I have ever known?

Then it hits me. That life wasn't a life at all. Becoming a part of The Forces wasn't my choice. Now I have the chance to do that. To start my life. To finally have a choice.

"I'm in."

Bea giggles. "Well then welcome, and please enjoy your stay."

———

The art of using a gun isn't that difficult.

It's not necessarily something you have to work at to become good. Almost anyone can learn how to work one—if they can get past pulling the trigger.

Whenever I pull the trigger, I pretend I'm playing a video game. The gun is just a game controller, and nothing I do while playing it affects my life. But I can't ignore the sound the bullet makes when it hits human flesh. It's like a crack, and then a scream, and then silence, which is the worst sound of all.

I'm sitting in bed, pondering this, while everyone else is out at The Lot. The Lot is this place where all the Awakened go out and party, which as Bea said, is a code word for lots booze, and lots of sex. Not exactly appealing, especially since I know Ezra's going to be there, and the last thing I want to do is be humiliated in a place I finally feel like I fit in.

But back to the guns.

I've been told I'm a very good shooter. Not because of my aim, but because when I shoot a target, I'm excellent at hiding my emotions. Most people cringe, or some people go as far as suicide because of the guilt of taking someone's life. But not me. I hide everything.

There are certain rules when you're a part of The Forces. One of them states that if one were to discover your identity, then you must kill them before they tell. No exceptions.

Obviously, Ezra's done so much for me through the little time I've known him. My killing him would be absolutely vicious. But what's worse is that my fear of him giving me away is stronger than anything else.

Maybe it's because of the terrible influences I've had in my life, but as I peer out the glass panes of the infirmary's small window and spot Ezra awkwardly grinding against Bea, I wonder just how easy it would be to pull the trigger on him.

I know it's him when I hear the familiar thump of his old combat boots. Reed's had them since he was little. I'm surprised his toes haven't become broken while trying to squeeze into shoes made for a twelve-year-old boy.

"Alia."

I'm still getting used to my surroundings, so it still feels a bit surreal to wake up and not feel the comfort of my mattress. The infirmary cot is terrible, but sleeping on the ground in Bea's tent sounds far worse, so I thought I may as well occupy the space since no one's using it. No harm, no foul.

"Hey, I know you're awake. Open your eyes."

Reed hasn't changed that much since I last saw him. That was what, maybe two, three weeks ago? He grew a goatee and he looks a bit paler than usual, but other than that, the exact same.

"Long time, no see."

He bites his tongue. I can tell he's pissed off; Reed never has a loss for words.

"I said be back at sunset with Cleo. How did you interpret 'go make friends with the enemy' from that? Honest to God, Alia." He sighs, and his voice drops to a harsh whisper. "You're our only female who scored an eight. We can use your strengths as our advancements. With a powerful woman on our side, our army is open to a whole other variety of capabilities. We can't risk losing you. You got that?"

"How did you get in here anyway?"

Reed shrugs. "Same way as you and Cleo. I lied."

I finally decide to suck it up and ask the inevitable. "Are you taking Cleo and me back to base?"

"I don't know." He scratches his chin. "Ubayy thinks it's very intelligent of you and Cleo to scout out a refugee camp for The Awakened. A lot of U.S. citizens have heard rumors about what's forthcoming, and some have taken the liberty of fleeing to other countries in search of safety. So, primarily, our main target is terminating the remnants, which by default will be The Awakened."

"What are you saying? You want me to stay here and kill everyone? That's insane."

Reed silences me. "A man is coming to this camp soon. He's one of them, one of the Awakened. He goes by the name of Hendrix. When he arrives, I need you and Cleo and Vinny to do your best to acquaint yourselves with him."

I'm confused. "Why is Vin here? And more importantly, what's with this guy that makes him so much more significant than everyone else?"

"Vinny's here with me to aid with the mission. I will also be spending some time here, trying to find any loopholes within this country's legal system, and so on. This should take a few weeks at most. As for Hendrix, we've managed to access some of the data stored away in the president's computer. We discovered some things."

"That's so wrong!"

"Our men are the strongest and smartest in this world. We fight with whatever we can get. If we're going to successfully carry out our plan for the ultimate vengeance, we need to do whatever it takes."

I swallow, my moral sense sliding down my throat and knotting up my insides. "Okay."

"So you agree to follow my commands?"

"Yes, sir."

"Good."

It dawns on me that I can't kill Ezra now; it was a foolish thought in the first place. But if the Awakened are all going to be maliciously threatened and slaughtered, they need every fighter possible.

When I eventually exit the infirmary, Cleo's outside my door waiting for me.

"Can I talk to you in private?"

I nod, and we head back into a small grove. The wind bites at my fingertips and I gingerly shove them in my pockets. Why had I stepped outside in the first place?

"I need to know why you followed me here."

Well this took an unexpected turn. "Reed told me to do it."

"Why?"

"Um, I don't know, maybe because you're never supposed to leave base unless you're instructed to."

"I came here because I want to help us fight back against a country that's taken so much from our people for so many years. You couldn't even say the same for yourself."

"Excuse me?"

Her eyes narrow into tiny emeralds. "I know you're not fully committed to The Forces, Alia. Rumors spread faster than wildfire when people get to talking. So I'm gonna be clear; you stay out of my way, let me handle Hendrix, and you never come into any form of contact with him."

I take a step back. "Why? What are you hiding?"

"I think the better question, Alia, is what are *you* hiding?"

She knows everything.

"By midnight tonight, Ezra will be dead." And with that final statement, she walks away.

Cleo's extremely clever.

She can find a way to murder someone and leave no trace of evidence behind. I feel like such a hypocrite for thinking this, considering yesterday I was plotting to do the exact same thing, but Ezra can't die. He's vital to the rebellion, and he's vital to the Awakened. He also appears very vital to Bea, seeing as I've caught them three times already today making out behind some bushes.

"Newbie!" Speak of the devil. Bea saunters into the infirmary, hungover despite the fact that it's 2:30 in the afternoon. "Your friend Eddie—"

"Ezra,"

"Ezra, whatever. He's so hot, oh my god."

"Bea, Ezra's going to die."

I end up telling her everything. But she's so drunk, I doubt she'll remember any of it twenty-four hours from now.

"Do you want to help me stop Cleo?"

She nods, her eyes glittering with mischief. "Let's rock this bitch."

Our plan was divine yet simple. Bea would be at The Lot with Ezra tonight, as usual. Quite a few people end up crashing in The Lot as they're too exhausted to move themselves, so Bea would "fall asleep" on top of Ezra in the open arena. If Cleo has any intelligence at all, she won't harm a hair on Ezra's head. If she shot him in the open area of The Lot, everyone would know she was the shooter. And everyone would know she's most certainly not a part of the Awakened.

After Bea leaves the infirmary, I can't shake the nagging thought of that computer data Reed mentioned earlier. He discovered something. Something big.

When most everyone is out and has left their belongings unattended to, I make my way to Reed's state-of-the-art trailer. It sticks out against all of the other campsites. Of course, Reed couldn't bear to live as a lesser being even for a few weeks.

Once I'm inside, I start searching through simple things, like drawers and cabinets, anything he could've hidden the data in. Soon I come across his briefcase, and I hesitantly reach in and come across a stack of papers.

Most of it I don't understand, but I do see five names printed in bold, which for the most part, isn't hard to comprehend at all:

Asher, Hendrix

Callahan, Ezra

Stone, Ever

Woods, Platinum

Wordsworth, Alia

Wordsworth, Alia. I carefully rub my fingers over each letter, wondering if I continue to do so for long enough, they'll go away.

I'll go away.

***

"What is this?"

Reed's face lights up with recognition, his face going stark. "What the hell are you doing? You can't go through my things like that!"

"You didn't answer my question. The list. Why is my name on it?"

He shakes his head and stalks toward me. "Hand it over, Alia."

"No!" I crumble it up and clench my fingers around it. "I want to know why my name is on this list!"

"Fine, you really wanna know? Sit down."

He walks over to his bed and peels off the scattered clothes, motioning me to come over. I take a seat next to him on the mattress. "Well?"

"You're one of them."

"I'm what?"

"The Awakened."

Time slows down for a second as his words hit me like a blade through the heart. I'm one of them.

I am Awakened.

"We didn't know it at the time when we took you. All we knew was that your father had turned against us. He was a part of the U.S. Army, though he had a tough time deciding his loyalties between our association and the United States government. In order to receive vengeance for his choice, if you will, we took his most prized possession. You.

"You look so much like your adopted parents, we figured it wasn't even a possibility that the child we had kidnapped was actually genetically modified to kill us. After your first health exam, though, it was clear. You had strength and intelligence far more advanced than any of the other children. You also had visions, which was a definite hint. All of the Awakened at some point in their lives have a foreshadowing of the future. A foreshadowing of what you are programmed to stop.

"We were going to return you to your home, thinking that we could not train someone who was trained to kill us, but Ubayy thought differently. He said you had no idea of the potential you wielded, and that we could instead use that potential to our advantage. So we did."

The visions. I remember those.

I was just three when the first one came. I was in the sandbox in my backyard playing with my mom. We were building a whole village in the sand when I saw it. It was fast, but so vivid and clear; people lying in the streets, dead. A woman, who looked like me now, was running up to them, pressing her head to their chests. When she couldn't find a living soul, she began to cry. I could feel her despair—she thought she had killed every one of them.

I had sobbed—seeing dead people is a terrifying image to a little girl. When I told my mom what I saw, she had merely told me it was nothing to worry about.

Now I know why. She knew. They all knew.

I realize I'm starting to hyperventilate, so I slow my breathing down. "You didn't answer my question. The list. What is so significant about those names?"

Reed gulps, averting my gaze. "This list consists of the top five targets."

"Targets of what?"

"This is a list of the strongest of the Awakened. You are our largest obstacles. We need you dead."

———

The minute the gun goes off, I know it.

Cleo killed him. Ezra's dead.

I take off for The Lot, sprinting as fast as I can in a pair of ragged sneakers. But when I arrive at the scene, the blood isn't pooled around Ezra.

The blood is pooled around Bea.

Cleo's aim was off. She's not as good a shooter as she thought. When she aimed for Ezra's head, she hit Bea's ribcage, which was positioned on top of Ezra's head.

My heart lifts for a moment, thinking *yes! Ezra's saved!*

But Bea isn't. She didn't even scream. She gasped for a second, then her eyes rolled back in her head.

"Bea!" I kneel by her side, pressing again and again on her chest, begging for her heart to start beating. It never does, though. And as I sit there, letting my tears fall on her lifeless body, I wonder if Bea is just the first of many deaths soon to come.

———

No one seems to even notice she's gone. It's like shootings happen all the time here. Maybe they do.

I'm too afraid to come out of the tent. I wouldn't want to risk coming into contact with Cleo or Vinny or Reed. Cleo seems to feel bad about what she did, but I'm sure it's just an act. She told everyone that the gun accidentally fired, and people seemed to believe her. I figured someone might be upset about it, someone close to Bea, but Bea's only friends seem to be Ezra and me.

Tonight's the night that guy Hendrix Asher is supposed to show up. It's possibly the only thing I'm looking forward to. He was on the list. Maybe he has answers.

I have to make sure Cleo doesn't get to him first, though.

As I walk outside my tent, I learn that I'm too late. Everyone's gossiping about the new guy who is reportedly sleeping at Cleo and Vinny's campground. Not many new people come in here, so I'm assuming it's Hendrix. Great.

I head out to The Lot later, guessing Hendrix came. Cleo probably dragged him out here, if anything.

I feel nervous, though I'm not exactly sure why. Maybe it's because my first impression on this guy matters. As I come upon his silhouette, I realize my hands are shaking. However, I can't afford to be this worried. If I want to be able to build a working relationship with Hendrix, I need to be fun and friendly. I plaster a wide grin on my face, and quickly exhale.

I approach him from behind. "Hey, your friends ditch you?"

He spins around, and I really see him for the first time. He's got dark, almost black hair greased back and the most beautiful purple eyes I've ever seen.

He finally speaks, with a deep, gravelly voice that most likely matches his personality.

"Aren't you freezing? It's like thirty degrees out here; I'm surprised it isn't snowing."

I giggle as if he just said the funniest thing in the world; I have to be flirtatious if I'm going to beat Cleo at her own game. "Yeah, a little."

He offers me his jacket, but I shake my head. "No, I'm fine. I'm used to it, really."

"Please, take it."

"I'm fine! Sorry, I'm not trying to sound rude, but really, I'm good."

He smiles. "You're okay. I'm Hendrix, by the way."

I smile back. "Alia."

Part 5

Ezra

They could never get enough.

It was always one more dose, one more pill.

The worst part was when their buyers would come to our house. It was never planned; some would show up at three in the morning, barely able to think straight. There was this time when I was eight, someone threw a rock through my window. It almost hit my head. Attached to the rock was a note with "cocaine" scribbled on it as if it were written by a small child. I handed it over to my parents, who were downstairs getting high in the living room. They scavenged through their pantry, filled shelf upon shelf with drugs and liquor, until they found what their customer wanted. I watched from the staircase, hiding behind the railing. It gave me comfort when I did that. I'd been supervising my parents for three years by then.

My dad was in a worse state than my mom—at least she could walk without falling over. My dad could not. He leaned onto her shoulder while she stumbled outside with her latest order.

They never came back.

I had quickly fallen asleep after they went outside; it was the middle of the night, after all. But when I walked outside in the morning, searching for them, I found their bodies hung from our oak tree like Christmas ornaments.

I didn't want to think that it was their decision to do that to themselves, so I blamed the drug addict who had come to the house the night before: I still blame him for their deaths. I wasn't sure what to do or who to call so I just ran. It was the cowardly thing to do, but I was a child, not a man by any means.

Sage came with me. We had met at school, when he was a third grader and I was a first grader. I've always been fairly introverted, so when a kid at recess started punching me, I just sat there and took it. It would've gotten bad if Sage hadn't pushed that kid to the ground. He even broke one of the kid's ribs from kicking him so hard.

We were instant friends.

I quit going to school once I finished the second grade; the whole concept just seemed stupid, and it's not like my parents cared.

Living on the streets wasn't exactly easy, especially in West Lake. We spent several years as nomads, with no resources except for the cardboard boxes and blankets we used as beds. We were too young to get jobs; we were desperate.

So we resorted to selling drugs.

It's a horrible job, I won't deny it. Your customers pay well, but business is busiest usually between one and five in the morning, so we had to sleep during the day in order to sell at night. Getting the drugs, however, wasn't hard. Before the bank took over the house after my parents died, I took everything. I thought there was a possibility it might come in handy someday. It was sickening, the amount and variety of drugs they had, but it was great for business. The money supplied us with good quality food and a decent wardrobe.

But then Sage changed. He was fourteen when he began abusing me. It started with little things, like calling me an ass. That I could handle. But it became an issue when he started hitting me. If I fell asleep on the job, a slap in the face. If I ran out of one of our "products," a punch in the stomach. It got to the point where I had to run. Again.

I ran to a local homeless shelter, where the owners eventually put me into foster care. I was adopted by a family, and for the first time I learned what a functional family was. They gave me hot meals three times a day and made sure I washed myself daily. They even enrolled me in middle school. I was still extremely shy, and shifted between friend groups constantly. But it was... normal. And comfortable, and safe, and secure. Life was good.

Up until I turned sixteen.

That's when they came. The visions, I mean. At first they came in flashes, and I thought they were fragments from dreams the previous night. But then I'd be sitting in English class, and suddenly, I wasn't. I was in a broken-down city surrounded by hundreds of dead bodies. I began to run from person to person, trying to get a signal of a pulse. I found none.

Shouts from my teacher brought me back to the present. He said that I started screaming unexpectedly, and sent me to the office for disrupting classroom behavior. It's not like I could defend myself. Who would believe me? So, they suspended me.

The visions tortured me. Sometimes they came at the top of every hour, sometimes they wouldn't appear for a month—but it was always the same thing. Repeated images of dead people playing in your mind is enough to drive anyone insane.

And it did. I couldn't sleep some nights, because the visions kept me awake, haunting my conscience. Just like right now, as I'm lying in bed. I get these premonitions right before they come.

They're coming soon. I brace myself, my knuckles turning white as I lay in bed grasping the sheets.

Someone's outside, I realize. I can hear their movements on the side of the house, and I can't stop myself from thinking, what if the visions are coming true?

What I see at my window is more surprising than if it had been a stranger.

Sage.

I haven't seen him for four years. We didn't end on a good note. Was he coming for revenge?

He raps on my window. "Ezra, open up!"

He looks worried. His rapping on the window turns into a hard punch, and the pane breaks, a sliver of glass slicing my left eye in the process. Shit.

"No time for explanations. We have to go. Placement has started."

"What are you talking about? I have a math test tomorrow; I need to sleep."

"You have to trust me. We have to leave now."

Has he gone crazy? "You appear in my bedroom at 2:00 a.m. after four years of no contact telling me we have to run away?"

"Trust me. Please."

I don't know how it happens, but the eight-year old inside of me appears. The one who, when Sage said to trust him, trusted him with all his heart.

"Okay. Let's go."

We ran. And we didn't look back.

***

"It felt like a flame had ignited inside my mind. I was sitting at the table eating breakfast when the first one came. All of a sudden, I was thrown into this other world. A world of horror and tragedy. I didn't even second-guess the logic of it; my instinct was to try and save their lives. I couldn't, though. I kept trying to, each time the visions reoccurred, but I could never manage to save a single life. I was too late."

Sage looks at me, his eyes wide and dark. We're sitting on the side of the road in the snow, freezing our butts off, with my hand pressed up against my eye. My eyesight is blurry but tolerable. I'm not sure why we're here on the side of the road, exactly. Are we supposed to be hitchhiking?

He finally speaks. "What if someone gave you an opportunity, not a good or bad one per se, and you just threw it away. Then you realized it's the opportunity of a lifetime, but by the time you tried to take it back, it was gone. You were too late."

"That sounds awful."

"I'm going to give you an opportunity. You either take it, or you don't."

"Is it good or bad?"

"Let's just say that if you take it, you could very well die. But if you don't, everyone around you will die. Now think about it—would you rather die surrounded by friends or live a long life of utter loneliness?"

When did Sage become so intelligent? I guess four years changes a guy. "That's an easy one. I'd rather die surrounded by my family and friends."

"So I'll ask you one more time; do you want the opportunity, or not? If you don't, I'll leave your life and you'll never have to bother with me again."

I sigh, hoping that what I'm about to get into isn't going to flip my life completely upside down. "Okay. I want it. I'm in."

He smiles. "Partners in crime once again."

I'm not sure if that's supposed to be a joke or not, considering we were actually criminals. Then Sage's phone rings.

"Sorry, it's my fiancée."

Fiancée? I keep forgetting he's twenty years old now.

"Hey babe. Yeah, we're on I-69. Okay, hurry. Love you."

When he hangs up, I start pressing him. "Will she be joining us on whatever this is?"

He nods. "Yeah. Her name's Iris. She's very intelligent, and good with technology, so she should be a huge benefit. Now shut up so I can explain everything to you."

This is getting more uncomfortable by the second.

"We're the Awakened. Your parents, the drug dealers? They were not your real parents. There was a major war back about twenty years ago, and your real dad was a soldier in it while your real mom was pregnant with you. He died in war, Ezra. The same people who killed your dad were eventually going to make their way here, so the president knew he had to take action before it was too late. He created The Awakened, which was genetically modifying fetuses before they began normal human growth. By the time the modified human reaches the age of sixteen, they will realize their superiority, and use it against the supposed enemy. But in order for this to work, the mother of the fetus has to sacrifice her own life, because the chemicals will kill a living, fully developed human. The visions are also a part of the process; they come as you're developing your unhuman-like characteristics, because it's what you're programmed to do later in life; save the lives of those who can't save their own. Your mom gave up her life, so you could take vengeance for your dad, and for your family; for everyone who will become a victim to these tyrants. Now it's time, Ezra. The enemies, which we call The Forces, are coming, and they are

189

determined to take over American civilization. You are the hope. I am the hope. Iris is the hope. The Awakened are the only hope for these people.

"I met Iris at the Government Mental Institution; it's not a place for the insane, that's just a cover. It's a place to contain people like us, so the government can examine our brains and begin their manipulations. We're not like their slaves, though; I mean, we give up some of our mind and bodily controls, but it's for a good cause. It's also where they kill the defects; the ones the modifications don't work on. Anyway, Iris and I were enclosed in the same cell. You get to know a person pretty well when you have no other social outlet.

"What I'm trying to say, Ez, is The Awakened are the only hope for these people. It's now or never."

A young woman appears from the darkness. She has long brown ringlets that glow in the moonlight, and a face like an angel, with creamy skin and narrow blue eyes.

"Hey, you guys ready?"

I am the hope.

I stand up and shake her hand. "It's now or never."

***

We spend several days wandering through never-ending roads. That's what it felt like, at least. I'm not even sure where we are, to be honest. All the roads signs begin to blur after a while, and all the names look the same.

We are no longer in the heart of New York, that I know; there are no buildings, but instead green grass and endless highways.

"We're almost there." Iris looks back to meet my gaze. She's the leader of this mission, and she's doing a damn good job at it. I'm surprised she ended up with Sage, actually, let alone wanted to marry him. She's so strict and determined to stay on task, whereas Sage couldn't care if it took us a year to accomplish whatever we're trying to accomplish.

"Baby, you have to let me rest, my feet are killing me." Sage collapses in the snow, and I can see his breath swirl in the air every time he breathes.

Iris rolls her eyes. Sage hasn't exactly been a great companion the last week. He complains about his feet hurting at least ten times a day, he never volunteers to keep watch at night, and the amount of times he asks "are we there yet?" is enough to drive a person crazy.

"Fine. Go lay down, and I'll discuss our next steps with Ezra."

"Thanks Iris, you're the best." He blows her a kiss and slumps down against the trunk of a tree, shutting his eyes as he does so.

Iris turns towards me. "Do you think he loves me?"

"What?"

"Do you think Sage loves me?"

I glance down at my feet, afraid that if I meet her eyes I'll end up telling her the truth. "Of course. He asked you to marry him. Isn't that what love is?"

"That's what I keep telling myself. He proposed, that's got to mean something. But the more I think about it, I feel like I'm just lying to myself."

"I don't really know—"

Iris starts crying, and I want to wipe the tears from her face, but I don't want to appear flirtatious. She's in a vulnerable state. "He didn't even give me a real ring. It was a promise ring, not an engagement ring."

"I'm sorry."

"Don't be." She gazes up at the stars. "We have to go."

I walk over to Sage and wake him up. "Hey. Let's go."

We trek the rest of the way in silence, and all I can think about is how a small part of me wishes I had wiped away her tears.

———

"This is it."

The building in front of us is nothing like I imagined it. I figured it would be some sleek futuristic dome like something out of a *Back to the Future* revival. But instead it's a tall brick structure with black windows and a tall black gate enclosing itself.

"Why are we here?"

Iris turns towards us. "This is where Placement is being held. The government tests our strengths and examines our weaknesses, and eventually they'll put is in a position in the army that best suits our specific traits."

Sage yawns. "Okay, so what now?"

"We go inside."

Iris' words are easier said than done. The security level is extreme, with guards surrounding every inch of the exterior walls.

As we approach one of the guards blocking the door, he gives us a menacing glare. "What do you kids want?"

Iris pulls her shoulders back in a strong disposition. "We're here for Placement, sir."

The guard shares a look of suspicion with his fellow coworkers. He gestures to one of them. "Jonah, escort them inside please."

The interior of the building reminds me of something like a modern day concentration camp. The halls are lined with masses of people, all dressed in the same navy jumpsuits. A terrible smell wafts throughout, a mixture between gallons of sweat and waste. Every face I pass looks at me with the same expression; fear. They're terrified. I can see it in their eyes— souls swallowed by merciless lies. Hope seems to be the last thing on their minds.

We finally make our way to two doors, which are tall and made of steel. Jonah opens them, and we slip inside.

A man sits at the head of a table. He's not the president, but he looks like someone who could be the president's right hand man. Another man, much younger, is seated next to him.

"How many are we missing?"

"Four hundred fifty-seven."

"Do we have their locations? Any form of identity?"

"It's hard to tell, sir. Some are easier to track down because they're in the area, but some are all the way across the country."

"Fantastic." The man rubs his forehead. "Hanson, you listen to me. We have less than thirty days before they come, if that. You heard of what just happened to the Syrians, and they are experienced fighters. This plan is going to go to shit if we don't have every single factor in place. Do you understand?"

Hanson replies. "Yes sir. But you can't expect me to track down five hundred people in two weeks. It's impossible."

The other man slams his hand down on the table surface. "Make it possible. Make it fucking possible."

"Yes sir."

"You're dismissed."

He finally notices our presence. "Who are you children, and why are you here?"

Jonah steps in. "Sorry sir, didn't want to interrupt you. They claim to be here for Placement. I thought I'd leave them in your hands." Jonah gives the man a nod, and curtly exits the room, leaving us to fend for ourselves.

Iris clears her throat. "We're a part of the Awakened sir. We're here for our Placement."

"Tell me your names, please."

"I'm Iris Wilkinson. This is Sage Pratt and Ezra Callahan."

He stands up. "Did you say Callahan? Ezra Callahan?"

I nod. "That's me, sir."

"Oh my god." The look on his face is one of shock, and my heart begins to beat faster by the second. "Hanson, bring the others in. Ezra Callahan's here."

***

The last thing I remember is the discussion with the man. Then everything went black.

My vision is hazy, but I can't rub my eyes to clear them because my arms are restrained. I try my legs, but they're shackled as well, effectively disabling me. I can feel wires on my head and I seem to be in a small white cubicle.

A voice comes through the ceiling. "Ezra, are you awake?"

It sounds like that Hanson guy from earlier.

"Let me out!"

"I'm afraid I can't do that, sir. Government's orders. Are you comfortable?"

"I don't give a crap about being comfortable. I want to know what the hell you're doing to me!"

One of the walls begins to slide open. Hanson walks through the door, looking exhausted with his wrinkled clothes and bags under his eyes.

"I can't tell you much, Ezra. But I can tell you that the government wants to contain you. They don't want you being Placed on account of the fact that they think you'll make some irrational decisions if you happen to… discover something."

"Discover what?"

"I can't tell you that. I've already said too much. Good day to you, sir."

Unbelievable. "Fuck you, Hanson! Fuck this government too! Fuck all of it!"

How is it possible my life has completely crashed and burned within the span of a few weeks?

I end up dozing off for a few hours. It gets boring after a while, being strapped to a chair with nothing else to stare at other than a white wall.

The walls begin to move once again, and I open my eyes. Iris enters.

"Iris! Oh, thank God, you've gotta help me out of this thing."

She clamps her hand over my mouth and whispers, "Shut it! I'm not supposed to be in here, I hacked their access code. I came in here to give you this."

She cuts the straps tying me down with her pocketknife, then sets a stack of papers on my lap.

"I'm not positive, but I think this is the reason why they singled you out. Examine those carefully, and make sure none of the government officials know you have them."

I nod. "Thank you. How's Sage doing, by the way?"

Iris dips her head, her dark curls cascading over her face. "Sage is dead, Ezra."

My heart stops beating, and it feels like the whole world starts to spin. "What?"

She finally meets my gaze, and I see tears running down her cheeks. "When they tranquilized you, he attacked one of the guards. Another guard shot him in the back of the head."

The feeling I got when I realized my parents had died strikes me again, a feeling as if someone just punched me in the gut. Sage was my rock; he helped my feel valued in a world where no one valued me. He was the only family I ever really had.

And now he's dead, because of me. Just like my biological mom. Dead because of me.

"I have to go." I don't even notice when she leaves, nor do I really care. He shouldn't have died. It's not fair for anyone to die when they're so young.

As much as I don't want to, I realize I better look at the papers Iris gave me. I probably don't have a lot of time before one of the guards comes in to monitor me.

At first, none of it makes sense. Half the documents are written in a language I don't recognize. I finally come across a contract that's written in modern English:

"Colonel Callahan has been taken hostage under the leadership of our tyranny. Mrs. Callahan, the wife who survived the Awakened operation has also been taken hostage. We will not return these American citizens to you unless you send us the Callahan offspring. We know of his power and worth, and he will be very beneficial to our people. Sign below if you agree to these terms."

"Hey, how'd you get loose?"

Hanson leaps towards me, but not before I manage to crumple up the papers into a large wad. Iris races in behind him and flails her arms wildly.

I throw the paper ball to her, and she catches it with ease, sprinting out of the room.

Suddenly, the walls around us open up. She hacked the system again. With my newfound freedom, I throw my body against Hanson's, slamming him against the ground. Fortunately, he's small, so that force alone was enough to knock him out.

We race into the conference room where the man we had talked to from yesterday was. Alarms are sounding all over the building, so it's only a matter of time before we're caught. We might as well make the most of it.

I yank open the doors and collapse once we arrive in the room. Sure enough, the man is in there, and turns to face us with an expression of horror.

"What is the meaning of this?"

Iris hands me the wad of paper, and I rifle through it until I spot the contract I read earlier.

"You knew!"

He folds his arms smugly and grins. "Mr. Callahan, I don't think you've thought this through. You see, whatever you have there, whatever you think could possibly be incriminating and somehow smudge the reputation of the government, will otherwise be ignored. That is a confidential file that is only able to be seen by a few selected eyes. Because you are holding that, you will get in very large trouble, young man. Jail time, or possibly much worse. But nice try, better luck next time." He laughs haughtily and seats himself back in his chair.

"I don't care. I don't care if you put me in jail for the rest of my life, but let's get one thing straight. My parents have been alive for the last sixteen years, and you don't seem to care whether they live or die." I walk out of the conference room and don't look back.

***

Atticus and Avril Callahan.

It's funny how we believe everything the government tells us. I wonder if anyone's even considered the fact that they could be lying to our faces, but we believe them just because they're wearing a badge. It's so manipulative.

Just like they manipulated the paperwork on my parents; Atticus Callahan, died in war. Avril Callahan, embryo donor. God, I'm so stupid.

I can't let anyone know, though. At least that's what Iris told me, and she's probably right. If I let anyone else know what I've discovered, it could spread around and lead to worse things. Reactions blown out of proportion, riots, who knows what else. I must keep a low profile, even if I've already kind of screwed that up.

I got the chance to look them up today. I wonder what it would've been like to have normal, biological parents as a young child instead of the drug dealers I got stuck with. Actually having playdates with friends, and staying in school, and my only worries being the math test during the coming week. How different it all would've been.

I know they'd be the kind of parents you hear about in books. They totally looked the part. In the pictures on the internet, my mom has dark brown curls, kind of like mine. And when she smiles, her blue eyes squint as if her eyes are smiling too. And my dad resembles the kind of guy who's friends with everyone, like a guy you'd go out and have a beer or two with just to get to know him better. My mom would make my lunch every day, and puts notes in my lunch box that say things like "Have a great day, sweetie." My dad would pick me up after school, and we'd play basketball until the sun goes down.

But I guess those parents really do only exist in books.

———

"Hey Callahan."

Iris's voice floats through the door, and I realize I have to wake up. They didn't know where to put us, so they found a large closet, threw some mattresses down, and told us to sleep.

She's already ready for the day with her dark ringlets compressed into a bun and sporting a clean sweatshirt and athletic shorts.

"What time is it?"

"Five in the morning."

"Why the hell are you waking me up then?" I throw my pillow at her and collapse back down on my mattress.

"I couldn't sleep." She glances at me with a sad look in her eyes. "I need someone to talk to. Can I talk to you?"

I yawn. "Sure. I might not pay attention though."

"That's alright." I listen to her breathing, slow and rhythmic. "I haven't really gotten to think about the fact that Sage is dead. And now that I have, well… I'm not as sad as I thought I would be. I mean, if we actually loved each other, wouldn't I be a lot more depressed?"

"I don't know, Iris. I've never been in love."

She laughs. "Doesn't surprise me."

"Thanks."

"There's this thing my mom always used to say. "'Humans tend to mistake words with thoughts.' Not everything someone says is what they truly believe or think. Anyone can say something. Few mean it. Words, often, are a mask hiding what someone's truly feeling."

"That's deep."

"Quit interrupting." She sighs, and I can tell I'm getting on her nerves. Well, that's why you don't wake me up at five in the morning.

Iris continues sharing her mom's wisdom. "This is why my Mom said the words 'I love you' are so tricky. You can say them over and over again until you even begin to believe them, and you can shout it to the sky for the rest of the world to hear. But in your mind you'll know. My mom would say, 'Your thoughts, Iris, are more important than any word. That's why your dad and I never say we love each other.' They just knew"

I sit up. "Your mom is an extremely intelligent woman."

Iris nods. "She was. Every time I told Sage that I loved him, I kept thinking, 'why am I saying this?' And most of the time, the answer was for self-affirmation. If you really love someone, you don't need spoken words. All you need is the silent chapel of your mind to have a mutual understanding."

"I whole-heartedly agree."

Iris looks at me again, and for the first time I can't find the shine that's usually in her eyes. They're dull. "What do we do now, Ezra?"

"What do you mean?"

A tear slips out of the corner of her eye. "We came all the way to this place in hopes of making some sort of difference. In hopes of following the destiny our parents laid out for us. But instead, we find out the government is filled with a bunch of manipulative assholes, your parents are being held hostage somewhere, and someone very significant in our lives is dead. The assholes out there have control over us. I don't see what else there is to do but surrender."

I grab her hand. "C'mon, don't talk like that. There are other options."

"Like what?" She lets her tears fall. "We have nothing left. This world is going to shit, and we're going with it."

And as much as I don't want to believe her, she's right. There's no hope.

The door is yanked open, and Hanson awkwardly steps in. His face is still wounded badly from when I lashed out at him.

"Ezra, Iris. Good morning." He nods. "Byron wants to see you both immediately."

Byron. So that's his name.

Iris and I are led to his chambers, a different room than usual. The ceiling is high, and it resembles that of a palace, with pristine wood glistening every inch of the entry foyer. The doors swing open automatically, and we don't even get the chance to take a step in before his big booming voice ricochets through our ears.

"Ezra, Iris, come in! There are some people I'd like you to meet."

***

"Hello our beautiful, healthy son!"

It's them.

They look a lot older than in the photographs online. Mom's curls are matted and frizzy, and her pretty blue eyes are lined with wrinkles. Dad's hunched over, but that doesn't stop him from smiling. He has a scar on his arm though, a fairly large one. I can't help but wonder what that's from.

"Mom, Dad!" I'm shocked. What do you say when you're meeting your biological parents for the first time after so many years? We share the same blood, but we're practically strangers.

"It's so good to see you, Ezra!"

"You too!" This is happening. I can hardly breathe.

"See, Ezra," Byron walks up in front of me, wearing a smug look on his face. "The government isn't bad. Your parents are perfectly happy and safe, not taken hostage. They're living perfectly content lives."

I stop for a minute. "Why didn't you just tell me that then?"

He raises an eyebrow. "Well, now what would be the fun in that?"

I shrug. "Whatever." I sprint over to my mom to hug her, but she steps away.

"I'm very ill right now, darling. Your father is too, and we don't want to get you sick."

That kind of shattered my heart. "I don't care. I've never met you guys, and I'm willing to hug you and risk getting sick... don't you want to hug me, too? I'm your son."

This is weird. Wouldn't most parents be hysterical after finally getting to see their son? Or maybe not. Maybe that's not how parents act. I guess I wouldn't know. I look back at Iris, and her brows are furrowed. Maybe she's noticing how weird this is too.

"Of course, honey! We care about you too much to get you sick."

"I guess that makes sense." I glance up at Byron. "Can I take them out to lunch or something? We have a lot of catching up to do."

Byron shakes his head. "Mr. and Mrs. Callahan unfortunately have to be leaving right about now. Besides, you're an important asset to us, Ezra. We need you for Placement."

"No. You can't just bring my parents here and hardly even let me talk to them! That's not fair!"

"My condolences, Ezra. Mr. and Mrs. Callahan, you'd best be off."

As they start to walk away, I can't resist. "Mom!" I run to catch up with her and set my hand on her shoulder...

But it goes right through her body.

"What the hell just happened?"

Iris grabs my hand. "They're holograms. Pre-recorded holograms they thought they could project in order to trick you into thinking your parents are here. When they're not."

I spin around to meet Byron's stare, and for once he doesn't look confident, but afraid. "You recorded my parents and transformed them into a hologram in order to make me believe they're okay?" I punch him. "You're a sick, sick man."

And with that statement, we sprint back to the closet and lock the door behind us.

———

"I actually had some hope when I first saw them."

"Hope for what?"

I sit down on the mattress and sprawl out my legs. "Hope that they were real. Hope that one thing in my life had actually gone in a good direction."

"That's why I stick by my life motto."

"Which is?"

"You hope for things, you get disappointed. Wise words from my brother." Iris sits down next to me.

"How come he believes that?"

She looks at me. "I guess it's because he was depressed. He never got the chance to experience the sensation of hope."

"Why?"

"He killed himself when he was sixteen. Those were his last words to me, and I'll never forget them as long as I live. At first I thought he was crazy, like those words were as loony as he was. But now I realize that they're probably the sanest thing I've ever heard. Because he's right. You hope for things, you get disappointed."

I nod. "Yeah. Weren't you hoping that coming here, to this place, would be our destiny?"

"I was."

"How come you didn't listen to your brother?"

She shrugs. "I thought not everything has to end up in disappointment. But it does."

"Where do you think they're at, Iris?"

"Who?"

"My parents. If they're not here, then where could they be? Are they actually taken hostage?"

"For all I know, Ezra, the government could've written up that contract themselves and planted it where I'd find it. Everything Byron's said so far has been a complete lie. I don't know what to trust anymore."

"What about us? What do you think will happen?"

"You want the truth?"

"Yes, please."

"I think we'll end up like everyone out there. All those people being Placed, manipulated by the government, families being ripped to shreds, and having no control over anything for the rest of our lives. We'll be forced to fight people who we're told are our enemies, when in reality, we are our own enemies. Every government official is supposed to be on our side but is actually against us, and there's absolutely nothing we can do about it."

I start to conjure up possibilities. "What if we retaliated?"

She shakes her head. "It won't work. They've got to be at least ten steps ahead of us. They know exactly what they're doing, and they're going to do anything in their power to keep us imprisoned here. They need us."

"So we just sit here and let them manipulate us like slaves?"

She stands up, as if the anger inside her is too much to contain. "No. We don't."

"I have one more question."

She sits back down. "Anything."

"Why is nobody trustworthy these days?"

"Society's like your parents, Ezra. Holograms. People can seem real and genuine, but most of the time, your hand goes right through them."

Iris lays her head on my shoulder, and we sit there quietly until the tug of dusk drags us into a restless sleep.

"Callahan, Ezra."

The door flies open and Hanson steps in. "We're ready for your Placement."

My heart starts beating rapidly at the word Placement. This can't be good. "Placement? But I thought I would have to wait a while. I thought I'd get some type of warning."

He beckons me to stand up. "You don't receive a warning. It's whenever Byron's ready for you. He's ready now."

Ready to Place me? Or ready to behead me with whatever can cause the most pain? I don't know at this point.

"Ezra!" He smooths the wrinkles out of his vintage tux and towers over me. "How was your evening yesterday?"

I gulp. "Fine, sir."

Byron smiles. "Good, good! You deserve nothing but the best."

He's being too nice.

"Hanson, please go fetch Lev."

"I thought you told me we were going to wait on getting Lev involved, sir—"

"Get him *now*." He then continues to smile at me, a wicked grin masking his true intentions.

"Let's proceed, shall we?"

"I guess."

"Fantastic. First, before you're officially Placed, I must get to know you better. So tell me, Ezra. Who are you? I want to know every last juicy detail!"

This is getting strange. But if I refuse to answer, I'll probably make him angrier than he already is. "Well, when I was younger I had parents who were drug dealers, until they were eventually killed by one of their consumers. After that I was an orphan, until I was taken in by foster parents. And now I'm here."

Byron strokes his chin. "You just told me about your family. I want to know you! Continue, if you will."

"Alright," I stammer. "When I was a kid, my life sucked. I dealt drugs, I hung out with bad people, and I basically had no hope that the world would get any better. After my parents passed, I was a wreck. But once I was taken in by these foster parents, life started to get better. I was happy for the first time in my life."

"What about Sage?"

"Huh?"

"Sage; were you close to him?"

"Of course I was." I think back to the first time we met. "He was my best friend."

"Did you agree with all of his actions?"

I answer truthfully. "I loved him, but no, I did not."

"I see." Byron scribbles something down on a sheet of paper, tears it, and hands it to me. "Please go to room 604B."

What? What's this about rooms? "What about Iris? Will we be in the same room together?"

He rolls his eyes. "Hanson, please escort Mr. Callahan out of my chambers."

Hanson comes up behind me and binds my hands with handcuffs so I can't fight back.

"Where are you taking me?"

"I'm going to shoot you now."

I don't even get a chance to react before everything in front of me goes dark.

———

When I awaken, I'm lying on a silver bed frame. There's not even a mattress, it's just a bed frame. I feel a sharp stinging in the side of my neck, and I realize Hanson didn't even bother to pull the tranquilizer dart out. Miniscule drops of blood trickle down my neck.

All around me are men, no women. That probably explains why it reeks like sweat and dirt in here. The walls look like they used to be white, but most of their surfaces are scuffed with black markings. The blue carpet is faded and ripping at the seams. But the worst sight is the people around me. They're all wearing the same black jumpsuits, and they look exhausted and like they haven't showered in days. They'd rather die than be here, I can see it in the way they move, with no motivation whatsoever.

"Excuse me?" I tug on the arm of a man walking past. "What is this place?"

"A deathtrap." He smirks.

"No I'm serious, I'm what you'd call... 'new' here."

He slowly nods. "Ah, okay. Well long story short, this is where they put the good ones. Congratulations, I guess."

"Wait, what do you mean the good ones?"

The man leans into whisper in my ear. "You're one of the stronger ones. When we go into war, they'll give you the hard job."

"What's the hard job?"

"Physical fighting. Shooting. Killing. That is, if you're not killed first." He laughs and hits my arm, then walks away.

"Wait, sir!"

"What do you want, kid?"

"What's your name?"

He spits out the tobacco he was chewing. "Lev."

Lev. What an interesting name. "I'm Ezra Callahan!"

"Don't care, kid." And he turns a corner.

His words continue to ring in my ears like a death threat, though. If you're not killed first? That doesn't sound very appealing.

"Hey," a group of guys approach me. "You're the new guy, right?"

"Yeah." After I answer, their faces droop.

"Shit, it's probably coming close, then."

"What's coming close?"

"Placement." He glares at me, as if this is somehow my fault. "They're getting all the Awakened Placed. It has to wrap up at some point, and then we're forced to fight."

"What if we don't want to?"

"Have you been living under a rock, kid? We're their slaves now. I've been here for two months, I'm pretty sure I'd know by now."

"Well, what are you going to do?" This is confusing me the more I try and understand it.

"You don't do anything, kid. We've tried. There's not a point." They too walk away, and I'm left more dumbfounded than ever. I hardly know where I am, and more importantly, where's Iris?

"Attention!" Byron makes an entrance, letting the large steel door crash behind him. "Room 604B. The time has come. Please, in an orderly fashion, follow me out this way."

And as I file out with the crowd, I get this sinking feeling that I'm about to meet my death.

***

We gather in a darkened room. There's a large board, lit up with projections of Byron's head on hundreds of news channels.

"Attention, American citizens! I am broadcasting to you live from every U.S. news station.

My name is Byron G. Wilson, commander of ONA. I was thirteen years old when I first began hearing about Operation New Awakening.

It was 2015, and my father was vice president. The president was going through a scandal, so my dad had to carry a lot of the weight of the nation on his shoulders. The day he received the letter had to be one of the scariest days of my life.

I was at home playing basketball with my brother when he stormed through the doorway. Normally, my dad had what you'd call a poker face. He always seemed cool and collected even when his world came crashing down.

But that day was unlike any other. His hair turned greyer and his face turned thinner and his eyes turned glossier. The dimple in his tie was loose and the cuffs on his shirt were frayed as if he had been fidgeting with them; it was a nervous tick of his. I knew immediately something wasn't right.

"Dad?" I remember asking. He was staring straight ahead at something above my head, but when I spun around to look, it was only the wall.

My mom entered the room. "How was your day at work, honey?"

He slumped on the couch like some kind of ragdoll. My mom gestured toward the staircase. "Go upstairs, boys."

"No!" My father screamed. "Let the children hear this. It involves their future too."

He gripped my arms and his knuckles turned white. "We're. All. Screwed."

My brother was only eight, so he had no idea what that meant. "You mean we're like nails?" He giggled but my dad did not find it amusing.

"No, son. We're all gonna die!"

"Jonathon," said my mother, "Let's discuss this in private when the children aren't here." She appeared calm despite the circumstances, but I could hear the waver in her voice.

"I don't care anymore, Diane! Who cares about the kids when we should really be digging our graves."

"Jon!"

He threw an envelope at her. It was yellowed at the corners with a drop of blood on the flap and the words scribbled, "To the U.S.A. from the Syrian government."

"What's this, Jon?"

"Your death warrant."

My mom opened the envelope with shaky hands. As her eyes scanned the words, I could physically see the blood drain from her face. "This has to be some sort of sick joke played by some kids. Teenagers can be so foolish."

"THIS ISN'T A JOKE."

My brother started crying and I walked with him to his room. But afterwards, I hid behind the staircase to hear everything my parents were discussing.

"What are you going to do? Let America die in flames? We're a country of freedom, Jonathon. We can't just surrender."

"Why not? Have you forgotten what happened with the Nazis all those years ago? A lot of people died, Diane. We cannot go through that again. And I don't even know the strength of these Forces or whatever the hell people are calling them. All the other leaders around the globe have said it's impossible to try and put up a resistance because it's not going to work. I am not sending our troops to a death sentence."

"Sometimes you have to take that risk, Jon. If you put this issue aside, you're going to regret knowing you could've done something, but you didn't; and out of what, fear? Is that really what being an American is about?"

I heard my father exhale. "I have an idea. It's a dangerous one, though."

Then I heard my mother say, "The only way we'll have a chance at beating this is if we do something dangerous."

He looked at my mother with narrow eyes. "Let's do something dangerous, then."

My mother finally noticed me behind the stairway. "Byron? Go upstairs!"

"No, Diane, it's okay. He's smart in science. I want him down here."

That was the best thing my dad could've said to me.

"What's your plan, Dad?"

"I want to genetically modify the human race so when the time comes, we are capable of putting up a fight against these asses."

My mom grabbed his shoulder. "Are you insane?"

I shook my head. "It's impossible to modify every human being, Dad. We're already developed. But there might be a way to modify a newly formed fetus. Scientists have been looking into it recently."

My father and I stayed awake all night, and every night for the next month doing research. It was a risky process; much of what we would discover had a fatal result in human development. Here is what we deemed possible."

A list in neon lettering suddenly projected onto the screen:

- Thought Process

- Brain Capacity

- Joint Movements

- Immunity (to illness or physical harm)

- Strength

- Increased Senses

Byron resumes talking. "We worked with some of the best scientists around the world and came up with a formula for a serum to test on a monkey fetus. The monkey was born brain dead.

For the next three months, we continued perfecting our serum until the next monkey fetus was born healthy and strong. There was a catch, though. The mother died soon after giving birth. This could not be corrected in the monkeys and it cannot be corrected in humans.

So yes, all the rumors you have been hearing about the New Awakening are true. It is real, and there are about 5,000 in the U.S. who have successfully become Awakened. Please, do not go into a panic, America. Yes, we have attackers approaching in a short amount of time; but that's what the Awakened are here for. They're here to save your life."

The camera goes black.

***

With every step, my heart is palpitating.

I'm not sure where they are leading us. We're walking through a narrow, dimly-lit hallway that resembles the passenger compartment of an airplane. It's about two feet wide. I'm sandwiched in between the guys in front and behind me.

It's like we're a bunch of drones. Nobody asks any questions; nobody dares to even try. We all just file out like mindless, obedient monkeys.

A strong odor has begun to waft around the tight corridors. Nothing about this situation is pleasant. I feel like I'm trapped in an endless maze, rounding corners leading to nowhere.

Finally, I can see a light up ahead! It's shockingly bright.

We are led into a fluorescently lit room with stark white walls and black chairs lining almost every surface. It's very sleek and modernized. Men in black are escorting people to their seats.

One of the men approaches me.

"State your name, current age, and place of birth."

"Ezra Callahan, age sixteen, born in Portland, Oregon."

"Please sit down in row EE."

I find the row of chairs with EE marked on them, and take a seat in the closest one. I spot the back of a familiar head a couple rows in front of me.

"Iris!"

She turns her head to face me. "Ezra! Come here!"

I'm about to stand up when one of the men walks over to me. "No moving, young man."

I point over to Iris. "I'm just going to talk to a friend."

"There is no time for talking to friends. This is a serious government matter, there is no room for play; do you understand?"

I give him a curt nod. "Yes, sir. My apologies."

"ATTENTION!"

I whip around to face the front, where a tall black podium has now been placed. Byron is standing behind it.

"Young men and women of the future, my name is Byron George Wilson. I am the primary reason why you are gathered here today."

A girl raises her hand.

"Yes, Eva?"

"Why are we gathered here exactly? You kidnapped me from my freaking house, my parents are probably worried sick!"

Byron holds up his hand as if to silence Eva. "That's what tonight is about. Tonight, in this very room, you will receive the answers to all of your questions, I can guarantee. Well, haste makes waste, let's get right to it!

"You are all here for one reason. Anyone know that reason?"

A skinny kid wearing glasses raises his hand. He looks more like he's twelve than sixteen.

"We're here because we're Awakened. We're genetically modified human beings who are programmed with capabilities that can save our nation from collapsing."

"Couldn't have explained it better myself, Ridley!" Byron claps his hands together. "You are here because you are the Hope. You are superior to our military, to our congressmen, to our president! And you know why that is? Because you, my ladies and gents, can save us all! You can avenge your parents' deaths; you can be our saviors!"

Everyone yelps with joy and begins to applaud. He's making this sound like we've won some sort of game show, when we're actually about to risk our lives with the whole country depending on us.

Iris raises her hand. "May I use the restroom?"

"Of course Iris!"

As she stands up she mouths to me, "Meet me in the bathroom."

I nod and raise my hand. "May I use the restroom as well?"

"Of course Ezra!"

I follow several feet behind her until we're out of everyone's sight.

"What's going on?"

She seems tense. Her breathing is rapid and her face is paler than usual. "We need to get out of here."

"What? How is that even possible?"

"Listen to me, Ezra. They're hiding things from us. Last night, when a guard fell asleep, I hacked into the computer of one of the receptionists here. Our parents are not dead."

"You're kidding with me right now."

"I'm not. Wait, let me rephrase that. A majority of the parents are dead. But not all of them."

"Are yours dead?"

"Yes. But here are the last names of the parents who are currently surviving."

She hands me a slip of paper. The handwriting is messy, probably because she wrote them down in the dark, but it's still legible.

Woods

Stone

Asher

Wordsworth

Callahan

"Callahan. Oh my god. Wait, how do you know for sure?"

"There was a document saved, titled Survivors. It wasn't exactly vague."

"I can't believe this. What do we do? We have to find these other people. Wait, shouldn't they be in that room?"

"Not necessarily. In fact, knowing how sly the government is, they probably have all of you in different locations."

"Why my parents though?"

"I don't know. But you're damn lucky. I know where one of the people on that list is, though. If you want to know, of course. I got her location from the computer."

My heart leaps. "Yes, who!? And where? I need to go find this person. Maybe they know something!"

"Her name's Alia Wordsworth. She's hiding out at this refugee camp for the Awakened."

"What refugee camp?"

"For people who don't want to go to war, who don't want to get Placed. You can't just go bombarding her with questions, though. You have to act like you don't know anything. Act like you're heading to the camp yourself, and casually become her friend."

"What does she look like?"

"Blonde hair and green eyes is all I got from the description." Iris comes closer towards me. "You should probably get going, you're going to need some time.

"And what about you? You'll be okay?"

She hugs me. "I'll be okay, Callahan. I hope someday, if we're both not dead and this is all behind us, we'll meet again."

I smile. "I'd like that."

I immerse myself into the chaos that is my life, and set off for camp.

Three Months Later

All I can see is white.

My eyes finally focus, and I take in my surroundings. I am imprisoned in an all-white room shaped like a cube, with seemingly no entrance or exit. When I try to move my hands, I realize they're handcuffed. I am also sitting in a chair, with which my legs are cuffed to.

I'm right back where I started.

I look over to the side. There are four other chairs next to mine, lined in a row, with three girls and one other guy who are also just now waking up. They seem as clueless as I am.

A girl with very pale skin glances at all of us. "Who are you guys?"

The girl next to her, with bright red hair, speaks. "I'm Ever Stone."

The guy next to her speaks. "I'm Hendrix Asher."

And finally, the blonde-haired girl next to me who seems familiar, speaks. "I'm Alia Wordsworth."

Then it's my turn. "I'm Ezra Callahan."

The pale girl speaks again. "I'm Platinum Woods. Does anyone know what we're doing here?"

I shake my head. "I don't know."

Then the lights go out.

"But I'm guessing we're about to find out."

Part 6

Platinum

Something is pounding against my skull.

When I finally muster the courage, I touch my hand to the painful spot near the back of my head. My fingers come away painted with blood.

I'm not sure how long I've spent in this room, with all of these strangers. Well, not all of them are strangers; the man with the purple eyes I've seen before, I just can't remember where. Everything from the last few months or so is a complete blur.

I ask them for their names, and when they respond, I feel a sudden connection to each of them. I'm not really sure why, or how. I just do.

The woman named Alia speaks up. "Since no one's going to take charge, I might as well do so." She's very pretty, and I can tell she's probably one of the tougher ones of the group.

"What is the last thing you can recall remembering? Blondie, you go first."

Blondie. Just like what Wren used to call me. "I fell off a building after I was shot in the head."

"Holy shit." The man named Hendrix gawks at me. "How'd you survive?"

"Because she's Awakened, idiot." Alia rolls her eyes.

"What?" That doesn't make any sense.

"You seriously don't know?"

"Know what?"

Alia spends the next half hour or so explaining to me what being Awakened means, and how I'm one of them. It all makes so much sense now. The brain scan, the president, my being able to survive after a bullet to the head, my parents… all of it connects.

"How do you know for sure, Alia? How are you so confident that we're all Awakened?" The girl with the red hair—I think her name is Ever—scowls at her. I can tell right away she's going to be kind of a bitch.

Alia pulls a crumpled up list out from her shoe. Sure enough, every one of our names is printed on it in in mocking bold letters.

"I stole this from a buddy of mine. He said this is the list that contains the most powerful and threatening of the Awakened."

I can't believe it. "It's us."

"Thanks, Captain Obvious." Ever glares at me, her green eyes flashing with what seems like envy. Geez, what'd I do to her?

Alia crumples the list up again. "Okay, back to our original discussion. Ever, what do you last remember?"

She thinks about it for a second. "I was running down a hallway when this shadowy figure reached out and grabbed me and shoved me into a body bag. That's my last really clear memory."

Hendrix's face turns a shade of stark white, then beet red. "Oh, god. I'm so sorry, Ever."

Ever's eyebrows furrow. "What are you talking about?"

"I was the shadowy figure that did that to you."

I can tell Ever's about to scream, but Alia silences her. "We can't make each other the enemy. We must stick together if we plan on making it out of here alive. Do you understand me?"

She nods. Alia points to Hendrix. "Your turn."

There's something between Hendrix and Alia, it's obvious. They look at each other with puppy dog eyes and sneak smiles when they don't think any of us arc watching. I wonder if they've met before.

"I was running away with Ever, when this guy stopped me and shot me with a tranquilizer dart. I went completely unconscious."

Alia nods. "Okay, my turn. The last thing I remember is I was at this refugee camp, when this guy named Reed also shot me with a tranquilizer dart. How about you, Ezra?

He clears his throat. "I was also at a refugee camp when my girlfriend got shot and died. After that, I pretty much blanked out."

Alia looks at him. "I miss her too."

Wait, this is getting confusing. "You guys know each other?"

Alia and Ezra give each other a sideways glance.

"I thought something was up. How many of you have already met? Because I know none of you."

"I know you because you were the girl my boyfriend kissed. I also saw you fall off that building." Ever looks at me.

My heart about leaps out of my chest. "Wren was your boyfriend? Also, we never kissed."

Hendrix interrupts us. "I saw you bleeding after you fell off the building. I thought you were going to die, but you made eye contact with me and I could tell you were going to be okay."

I smile. "That's why I recognize you."

He smiles back. "I also know Alia. We met at the refugee camp."

Alia smiles. "Not only do I know Hendrix, but I also know Ezra from meeting him at the camp."

It dawns on me just how weird this is. We've all been living separate lives, meeting each other and not thinking anything of it, only to come together in the end. It's fate.

Suddenly, an automated voice ricochets throughout the room. "Platinum Woods, a government official has requested your presence at this time."

Then the floor below my chair begins to descend and I am taken down into a pit of darkness.

Wren is there when I open my eyes.

We look like we're in a warehouse. Several guards begin to untie my wrists and legs, and when they're finished I sprint over and throw my arms around him.

"Platinum!"

"I missed you so much." I don't hold my tears back, but he wipes them from my cheeks and kisses me on the head.

"I missed you more."

"You have fifteen minutes, Ms. Woods."

I nod at the guards and they walk away to give us some privacy. There's a small, ragged sofa in the corner of the room where we sit down.

"How are you?" His hair has some grey streaks in it, and he looks exhausted.

"No."

"No?"

I shake my head. "I don't want small talk. I haven't seen you in months! Tell me why you're here. Tell me why you have a scar shaped like Europe on the side of your neck. Tell me in full detail how much you've missed me, and don't leave any of it out. Tell me what caused some of your beautiful curls to turn grey, and what formed those bags under your eyes. I have so much lost time to make up with you, and I'm not wasting it with a conversation about how I'm doing."

He's quiet for a moment, until his lips touch mine and all the time we lost is made up for in that fraction of a second before he leans toward my ear.

"They're going to kill you. You have to get out of here."

"Ms. Woods, your time is up."

And as my hands are cuffed again and I ascend towards the sky, I wonder if I'll ever get to see him once more, or if the next time we meet, it will be at my funeral.

It's been three days since we've all found ourselves trapped in this room together.

They haven't fed us or given us any source of water, but for some reason none of us have any desire for it. They must've given us something that would sustain us from needing any nourishment.

It hasn't been too terrible so far. Ezra and Hendrix are pretty cool, despite Hendrix's stuffing me into a body bag several months ago in an attempt to rescue me. I've hated Platinum from the moment I've laid eyes on her, but I'm trying to not let it show because of Alia's stupid "we can't turn against each other" rule. But c'mon, Platinum isn't even pretty. I'll never understand how Wren thought she was somehow better than me in any way.

I don't like Alia very much either. I know she's trying to take charge and everything, but there's not much you can do when you have no idea where you are and your hands and legs are handcuffed together. Honestly, she needs to chill.

Suddenly a door opens where I didn't even know there was a door. It's camouflaged in the wall shockingly well.

Oh my god.

"Ever Stone." Dreyden nods at me when he enters. "You're needed for a health examination."

I don't even hear what he says. Those brown eyes have already lost me.

Two men come in and unstrap me from chair, but then cuff my hands again once I stand up. They flank me on both sides, as Dreyden leads me to a solitary room that is also all white except for a black examination table. I sit back on the table and wait for him to shut the door.

"You didn't tell me you worked here now."

"You didn't tell me you were scheming to escape with Mr. Asher."

"I wasn't."

"Ah, I see." He pours a vial of liquid into an injection pen. "It's definitely not a coincidence that you were stationed right next to him back in the hospital."

"He was in a freaking coma!"

"Like I'm gonna believe that."

Anger courses through my veins. What a jerk. "I can't believe I ever thought of liking you!"

As the words spill out of my mouth, I realize just how stupid I am.

Dreyden sets the vile down and turns around. "What?"

I shake my head. "Nothing. But let's set the record straight here, buddy. I'm not the only one with dirty little secrets here. A little birdy told me the government's planning on killing everyone who's trapped up in that room upstairs. That's a pretty big accusation, wouldn't you agree?"

"I'm not allowed to talk about confidential information."

"So it's true."

He narrows his eyes, and I can practically see flames burning within them. "Damnit, Ever. You're so nosy and you never know when to just shut your mouth."

"All I want to know is why we are different! Why everyone else is getting Placed right now and we're being caged like wild animals!"

"It's because you are!" He runs his hands through his hair, cursing himself.

"What are you talking about?"

He sits down, sighs, and gives in. "We call you the Untamed. Everyone else is classified as Tamed, or other words, correctly modified to fit our standards for Placement. They're obedient and they're loyal, and they can fight on command. That's how they were programmed. That's how everyone was supposed to be programmed."

My heart is sinking. "What happened with us, then? Why are we Untamed?"

"The Glocylic serum is injected into the mother's womb along with a number of other mutations in order to modify your DNA. There was only a ninety-nine percent success rate, however. When the serum reacted to your DNA, it made you stronger than we ever could've thought possible. It made you almost unhuman. Part of this passed onto your mother, and she became stronger as well, which means she successfully resisted the genetic modification."

It takes me a moment to process everything. "Are you telling me my mother's alive?"

"After your birth, your mother had the serum inside of her, so she was smarter and more powerful than she knew she was capable of. The nurses put her into a body bag, assuming she would quickly die just like the other women. Instead, when she was alone, she snuck out of the bag and the hospital. She was searching for answers about her husband's death. She flew to Germany, where her husband had supposedly died, and she discovered him being held hostage by The Forces."

"What did they do?"

"They ended up escaping, went undercover for a while, and found some things out. Dangerous things that if I ever told you, the president would probably kill me with his own two hands."

That's it. I leap off the table and press my hands around his throat, cutting off his oxygen. "Tell me or I swear to God I will kill you right here, right now."

Even when his face turns a dark shade of blue, I hold on tight. Then he waves his hand in a surrender. I let go and let him cough it out.

"Okay," he stammers, clearing his throat. "I'll tell you. You've been informed correctly; everything about how The Forces have been dominating world control. But haven't you noticed it's a little off how they've never once targeted America?"

"I guess."

"Not all of the Awakened are being Placed for war."

I'm still confused. "What? Why else would they be Placed?"

"The ones the government deems as fit enough, or Tamed enough, will be trained for war. The Untamed, such as you, are going somewhere else."

"Where?"

"The president's been holding The Forces off for as long as he can. He's been sending the Untamed to The Forces so they can use them for their army. When your dad was fighting over there, he never died. The Forces saw him as valuable, so they were going to use him as one of their own."

My heart is going to burst out of my chest. Somebody's stolen my lungs and I can't breathe. "Why would they send their strongest to work for the enemy?"

"It's a bribe. We send them our strongest weapons; they hold off their attacks."

I can't believe this. "What does this mean, Dreyden?"

"In a month, you're going to be shipped off to work for The Forces, and there's nothing you can do about it."

Today marks a week.

Everyone's been acting strange. Platinum's depressed, and Ever seems spooked. We've tried to get her to say something, anything, but she's silent.

I can't handle the quiet any longer. It's mocking me, while compressing all the noise that needs to be heard. "Platinum, Ever, I know you guys know something, so why don't you just come out and say it."

Platinum shakes her head. "I can't—"

Then it's like a soda can explodes inside of me, and I come fizzing out at the seams. "Damnit, I don't care anymore! I'm sick of being trapped in this room while my dignity slips away through my fingertips. I don't give a shit how much it pains you, we're all going to die unless one of you can explain yourselves!"

"Our parents are alive."

I think Ever's lying at first, but when I look into her eyes I know she's telling the truth.

"We're called the 'Untamed.'" She meets my gaze. "We're the dysfunctional kids. The ones who were born with too much power for their own good. The government's been withholding The Forces all this time because they've been sending teenagers like us off to be slaves in exchange for peace."

A feeling of dread crawls up my spine, squeezing it until I swear I hear the bones snap in half.

Ezra furrows his eyebrows. "Alright, well that's a lot to process at once. But how does that have anything to do with the fact that our parents are alive?"

Ever starts talking again. "The unhuman capabilities spread to our mothers as well. They lived after our births, and ended up escaping. My mom found my dad in Germany, and he wasn't dead, he was being held hostage by The Forces."

"So you're telling me that our fathers weren't actually killed in war, but that the government just used them as pawns to get what they wanted?" Alia shouts. "They lied to five thousand women about the deaths of their husbands?"

"Hey, you have no right to talk." Ezra looks at Alia.

That was a weird comment. I wonder if he knows something about her.

"What happens now, Ever?" asks Ezra.

"Nothing happens." She blows a red lock of hair out of her face. "We're being sent off as hostages too. There's nothing we can do about it."

"There has to be something." I rack my brain for any sort of idea, but nothing comes to mind.

"Do you see what's around our hands and feet, Hendrix?" Platinum responds. "How could we possibly fight back and make any sort of change at all that could save us from this disaster?"

I don't reply.

Hours go by, and we're all so lost in our own thoughts, nothing is said.

Alia's been crying for four straight hours. I'm surprised; she has such a tough demeanor, I never viewed her as someone who could ever let her guard down.

"Hey," I whisper. "It'll be okay."

"But you don't get it!" she screamed. "They lied! My dad's been alive and I never knew! God, when did my life become such a wreck?"

I gaze at her sympathetically. I care about her so much, and I want her to know she's going to be okay. "I know. But at some point you have to stop holding in all that anger. You have to stop being so sad and killing yourself over this. Yeah, a lot was screwed up fifteen years ago, but you have to realize that the past is the past and it's impossible to change because it *happened*, Alia. But don't mess up your future because of someone else's mistakes. Start being gentle with yourself. At some point you have to start spreading love and happiness instead of being terrified of the consequences it all could bring. You must love yourself, and love those around you before it's too late. We have to make the best of the situation we're in. Don't waste away the hopefulness of life on trivial things; it does no good, and you only regret it in the end."

She wipes her nose. "I appreciate what you're trying to do here, Hendrix, trying to put a positive spin on all of this. But my life is beyond fixable, and my problems are anything but trivial."

Seeing Alia in this state strikes me as an odd parallel to myself. Consistently boxing myself into a world of pain, never once searching for a way out of the hell my father put me through. But I've learned from that; sometimes you have to burn down the sources of your pain in order to discover a new beginning. You have to stop looking at the flames and focus on what's beyond.

As I look around at this room of people, I finally realize that they've all been looking at the flames for so long, they've lost hope. It's like watching somebody climb a hill, and when they're almost at the peak they start tumbling down. That's what's happened to all of us. We've lost our control, we've lost our pride, and so we've lost our faith in that we'll ever make it out of this room alive. As much as I hate to admit it, we've let the government get to us, and let them rob us of the humanity we thought existed. It saddens me to see the rest of them like this. I just wish there were something I could do to lift them up.

None of us asked for this. None of us asked to be different. None of us asked to be Untamed. Why should we have to be put through all this crap?

And then there's Alia. Sweet, beautiful, innocent Alia. The golden-haired girl with the sparkly eyes that look like emeralds and the smile that beams a ray of sunshine. I can't let her endure this. She's too fragile.

When dawn arrives the following morning, I decide that someone needs to take action around here. I can't let them go down like this; not without at least trying to save ourselves. And if they don't agree, fine. I won't save their sorry asses if they don't want to be saved.

Once everyone's awake, I make sure I have their attention. I can see Alia's eyes light up when I say I have an announcement.

I decide it would be better to whisper, just in case we're being monitored, which I assume we are. "Tomorrow, I'm going to attempt an escape from this hell-hole. If you'd like to join me, great. If you don't, fine. But I'm leaving with or without you."

I bleed in a field of desolate trees and vengeful blades of grass.

The sounds of cars driving on an invisible highway catapult into my ear drums and never seem to leave. Charcoal clouds lurk above, running to catch me as I barely miss their grasp. The rain drops are bullets, piercing my skin with such a burn that screams come crawling up from my lungs and never cease. None of this fazes me, though. Not at all. It's the darkness that terrifies me. It's the black empty void filled with shattered shadows and sulking stars that have lost their shimmer, and it clenches my heart with an inexplicable sadness.

Until I see the light.

Its whiteness blinds me, a million sparkles in the midst of all this darkness. A speck of good in a world of evil. I never thought the world would ever be rid of evil; I never thought I would be. But here it is, a hopeful hand reaching out in a land where hope is rare and those who help are few.

But before I reach its fingertips, it's gone.

"Alia! Wake up!"

My eyes burst open to see Ever hovering above me. It takes me a moment to get back into reality. The dreams never stop. The horrifying moments of my childhood replay in my head repeatedly, night after night like some awful record that never stops spinning. Not all of them are bad, though. Sometimes there's a light at the end, and that light gives me hope. I'm not sure why, it just does.

Ever shakes me again. "C'mon, hurry up!"

I finally notice I'm lying on the ground. When I glance up, I see all the chairs still lined in a row, but the ropes on them are sliced. I'm curious as to how, until I spot the pocket knife near one of the ropes.

"How'd you get that knife?"

"A guard came in," spoke Ezra, coming out from the darkness. "He came to check on whether my ropes were secured, and I kicked him where the sun don't shine. I threatened to do it again if he didn't give me his pocket knife." He smirks.

"Quit bragging and get your ass outside," Ever prods him and he quickly walks through the door.

I don't move.

"Hey Blondie, you coming or what?"

Something inside me is hesitant. "I don't know."

Ever runs a hand through her hair, and I can tell she's stressed and I'm just adding to her irritability. "Why not?"

"I guess I'm just scared. I know I seem like this badass warrior chick who has no fear, but that's because I've always known what's next. That's the life I grew up with. I was living in a routine," I stutter for a minute. "But now I don't know what's next."

"Hey," Ever puts a hand on my shoulder. That surprises me. I didn't think she had a compassionate bone in her body. "There's this thing that I learned recently. About life, I mean." She loses herself in her thoughts for a moment. "If you keep living the same way every single day and never do anything different, that's not living. That's nothing. You wanna be nothing?"

I shake my head.

"Then don't be. Life comes with no guarantees. If you're afraid of change, then you will never live. So don't live in fear, live on it. Take risks and live every moment like it's your last, because you never know when that will be. Yeah, this whole thing has pretty much sucked, but hasn't it given you a purpose? Hasn't it given you a sense of adrenaline and thrill and excitement? That's what living is, Alia. Living is stepping out of your comfort zone, hanging onto the edge, and getting that rush of energy through your veins every single day. You've come this far. Don't give up on the rest of us. But most importantly, and as cliché as it sounds, don't give up on yourself."

She takes my hand, and I smile. "I think that's the nicest thing I've ever heard you say."

She smiles back. "Just because my last name is Stone doesn't mean my heart is one."

With adrenaline pumping through my veins, I sprint out the door, for once excited that I don't know what's next.

It happens again.

The bullet hits my leg. Out of instinct, I fall down, a scream leaping from the back of my throat. The others look back at me, and Platinum comes racing to my side. "Are you okay?"

I start to say no, but then I realize there's no pain. Just like when I was little and got shot in the courtyard, I feel absolutely no pain. Being Awakened has its perks. Being Untamed has even better perks.

I stand back up, much to the surprise of the others. "Let's go."

The guards continue to shoot, and we continue to dodge their bullets. I thought maybe once we escaped the white cubicle we'd find ourselves in some sort of laboratory. I couldn't have been more wrong; it's practically a maze of white cubicles. Stark white hallways leading to nowhere. That's what it seems like, at least.

"Stop where you are, or we'll kill you!" That comment makes me laugh. They have no idea.

Hendrix keeps tugging on the handles of every door we come across, but none of them open. I can tell he's getting pissed, and that's the last thing we need right now.

"You did it!" Platinum screams. And sure enough, a door opens.

"What's inside?" asks Ever.

"Another door." Hendrix's eyebrows furrow, and he cautiously steps into the room and analyzes the door. "Why have a door that just opens to another door?"

"Shit, they found it!" One of the guards yells from down the hall, and I hear a dozen footsteps running all at once.

"Open it!" Ezra urges.

The footsteps are nearing rapidly, and I'm positive that we're not going to make it. Hendrix flings the door open just as I'm about to shut my eyes and raise my hands in defeat.

Until I see the light.

All I know is that we're somewhere in Germany.

I'm not sure where, exactly, but this is Ever's idea. She seems to be the only one with a slight sense of purpose out of the group, so we all followed her lead.

We raced out of the building with nothing but the clothes on our backs. We assumed there would be shots fired or something to try and keep us from escaping, but not one person tried to stop us. We ran until we reached a nearby bus station. Fortunately, we found enough loose change in our pockets to pay for the bus fare to the airport. After an agonizing thirty-minute bus ride, we arrived at the airport. It wasn't as easy once we got to this point. We chose to go to the airport because it was our fastest route out of the country, but we didn't think through all the logistics. Most of us got past security just fine, but Alia was stopped in her tracks. One of the guards looked at Alia and then looked at The Forces' wanted poster hanging near the security checkpoint.

"Excuse me, miss." One of the guards had said. "Please stand in this identification scanner for a moment."

The guy scanned her face. Fortunately for Alia, the photograph on the wanted poster was too blurry for a good comparison to the scanner's photo, so the guards let her pass through security.

Another difficult aspect of the operation was paying for tickets. Alia, however, knew a loophole. Through one of the communal computers in an airport café, she was able to hack into the airport's system and retrieve five tickets without having to pay a dime. How she did it, I'm not sure. She claimed to have had a lot of experience with electronics in the past. After that, we hopped on an excruciating nine-hour flight to some unknown town in Germany, and wound up at a dingy bed and breakfast.

Alia tugs on the cuff of my sleeve. "You wanna go step outside for a second? The guy sitting next to me reeks of smoke."

I look over to see what the others are doing. Hendrix and Platinum are playing pool, and Ever's flirting with some twenty-something dude. "Sure, it might be nice to get some fresh air." Staying in a bedroom attached to a bar sucks. The sheets on the bed smell like they've been doused in a heap of cigarettes, and the carpet has a strong liquor odor to it.

She laces her fingers through mine and we step outside, sitting on a curb with the only source of light being a dim lamppost towering above us.

Then I look at the moon, and notice how its beams shimmer upon Alia's face like a spotlight. Why wouldn't they be shining on her face, though? She's special. If adventure was a physical form, she would be it. She looks like ominous undergrowth luring you towards itself so it can wrap its tendrils of vines around your soul and there's nothing you can do but admire its mysterious beauty. She smells like Niagara Falls, a shocking white mist that robs you of your breath but gives you a sense of clarity like none else you'll ever receive. She smells like the sweetness of the stars and the bitterness of the night, but never, ever, ever like home. And that's a good thing.

That's the moment I realize I'm in love with her. We might be going through some crazy shit, but I love her. That's all that matters right now.

249

"I haven't looked up at the sky in a really long time," she whispers.

"Yeah, me neither."

"It's so infinite."

I notice her shivering and put my arm around her. I can feel her muscles tense, but then she relaxes into me.

"I guess we've been so caught up in everything going on, we haven't had time to care about the simple things in life."

"Yeah," she agrees, and kicks at a pebble with her toe. I glance back up at the stars.

She starts talking again. "We're so small, compared to these stars, the sky… to everything, really."

"We are."

She leans her head on my shoulder, her eyes still fixated on the sky. "You know, if people stopped to look at the stars sometimes, I bet we'd live our lives a whole lot differently. When you look infinity in the eyes, it's like nothing else matters. Nothing but you and the stars."

Silence encloses us, and we don't talk anymore until a very drunk Hendrix prods us with a stick and demands we come inside.

Morning seems to come only seconds after I fall asleep. The sleeping situation is unfair. The girls claim they need their beauty sleep, so they take over the king-sized bed while Hendrix and I are supposed to get a satisfying rest sleeping on the wooden planks that make up the floor.

Ever, Platinum, and Alia all come out of the bathroom at once. For the first time in the last couple months, they're clean. Ever's hair is no longer a muddy auburn but a bright red, and Platinum's skin doesn't look as pale. Alia's even become prettier, if that's possible. Her golden hair is almost blinding, it's that shiny.

I also notice they're dressed in clothing that blends into the German society strikingly well.

"You gals Germans or something?" Hendrix laughs and points to their outfits.

Ever scowls. "Very funny. Adalhard gave them to us."

"Who?"

"He owns this place. He also sells clothing for pretty fair prices, so unless you wanna stay stuck in those grimy hoodies of yours, I'd suggest buying some. It's also better we blend in, anyway. Less of a chance we'll get caught."

After Hendrix and I purchase our own German outfits, we all head outside in the uncomfortable cold weather of February.

"So what's our plan?" Platinum asks, looking primarily at Ever.

"Well, our parents are here, so I think our first goal should be to find them."

"How do you know for sure?" Alia furrows her eyebrows. "Our mothers came here sixteen years ago, Ever. How do we even know if they're in Germany? How do we know if they're even alive?"

Ever groans. "God, Ms. Know-It-All, have some faith in me alright? I might actually know something you don't."

"Do you?"

"Um, yeah. I have an ally, you see. Someone on the inside." She pulls out her cell phone and Dreyden's face pops up onto the screen through video chat.

"Hey guys." He waves from inside some sort of laboratory.

Ever smirks. "Dreyden's our key. He works for the government, he knows all their secrets, and most importantly, all their weaknesses. We can figure out the truth behind all of this, and stop them from sending us to The Forces to be used as their slaves."

Hendrix interrupts her. "I don't know if you realize this, Ever, but if they don't send us away, The Forces are going to come here and kill us anyway."

"That's where you're wrong," says Dreyden. "Germany is one of The Forces' multiple headquarters. If you can stop them before they even get the chance to come over to the U.S., you'll be safe."

"That's impossible." Platinum glowers. "There are five of us and probably hundreds of them."

Dreyden shakes his head. As much as he denies it, I can clearly see the crease of worry visible on his forehead. "You're right, it's going to be risky, and your lives are at stake. But you either suck it up and fight like you were created to do, or you can be sent off to work for the enemy."

I realize he's right. This is what we were created to do.

"I'm in. Let's do it."

It's been five days.

The last few days have been nothing but torture. The headquarters are in Berlin, and we're in Bremen. It's not far, only about four hours via car, but walking is taking longer than we'd hoped. If only the weather was nicer, and we wouldn't have to keep sleeping on the cold remains of snow littering the grass.

It hasn't been all terrible, though. Germans are super friendly, and they always pass us with a big grin while saying, "*Guten Tag!*" I'm not sure what it means, but I smile and wave anyway. I feel like no one's been genuinely nice to me ever since this started four months ago, so it's a good feeling.

"You should be approaching your destination shortly," I hear Dreyden say from Ever's phone. "Only a little farther. Look for a sleek black dome structure. That's what this map says, at least." Dreyden stole a map from one of the president's files, which describes the general location of all the headquarters they've discovered.

"Okay, but where—" Ever stops dead in her tracks. I'm about to ask why, but then I look up.

There are those moments that change your life forever. Sometimes those transition moments are so subtle and seemingly pointless you never even sense it, but this moment is practically waving its hands in front of my face, it's that huge.

Imagine the largest building you could ever fathom. But imagine it as a dome, jet black with the sun's rays bouncing off it and blinding anyone who dares to lay their eyes on it. That's this building. It's beautiful, in a strange way, but also horrifying.

I'm surprised they would plant such a structure in a busy place, until I see the twenty-foot high fence enclosing the property, not to mention guards standing dutifully in front of the fence. The sign outside reads *Ausbildungsgesellschaft für Kriegsdienst-Offiziere*.

"What does it say?" I ask.

"War Officer Training Corporation, roughly translated." states Alia. I'm not even going to ask how she knows German.

"How do we get in?"

"Shut up, don't talk so loud, the guards might hear you." Whispers Dreyden. "Ever, do you have your Bluetooth on you like I told you to bring?"

"Of course." Ever pulls out a small metallic chip from her pocket.

"Hook up your phone to the device. That way you can still hear me, but the guards won't be able to." After Ever does this, we all lean in to hear Dreyden's instructions.

"I told Ever what to pack before you guys left, so she should have all the supplies. First, you need to sneak to the back of the dome. The bars around the fence were built looser back there."

"What about the guards?" says Hendrix. "They have guns; they can shoot at us."

Ever pulls out a bag of tranquilizer darts.

"You brought tranquilizers?"

She nods. "Of course, it'd be dumb if I didn't."

Dreyden clears his throat. "Once the guards are down, you should be able to get through the fencing with the saws I gave you. I got them from the stock of army weaponry and they can cut through anything. After that, you'll reach the back door. Enter in the code 9452, and the door should unlock. There will be more guards inside, but that's what the tranquilizers are for."

My heart begins to pump rapidly, almost out of my chest. This is it. This is what I've been fighting over since I was first caged in that cell all those months ago. "Guys," I say, and they all turn to me. "Look, maybe we haven't known each other long, and maybe we're all walking straight into the arms of death, but somehow fate has brought the five of us together on purpose. And I just wanted to say that if I die, I'm proud to die surrounded by you all. Thank you." I grab Ever and Alia's hands. "I love you guys."

With those final words, we load our tranquilizer guns.

The feeling of shooting someone is weird.

At first all this power surges through you and you're on top of the world, but then your heart plummets as you watch the life die out of their eyes, because you know it was you that did that to them. As the tranquilizer dart goes through the arm of the first guard, it's all I can do to hold back tears. I can tell the others feel the same way, except Alia, she shoots them down like it's nothing.

"How are you so content with this?"

"I've got some experience that I'm not very proud of." She gives me a curt nod and I don't question her any more.

I watch the guards fall like dominoes until there are bodies piled on the ground like a heap of snow. Ever rummages through her backpack until she pulls out a large saw. The edges are so sharp they remind me of shark's teeth.

"This should do the trick." Ever smirks and presses the blades to the fence, but predictably, The Forces planned for a situation like this. It takes almost an hour to saw out a hole large enough for us to squeeze through.

It only takes ten seconds after we step onto the grass for the alarm to blare, red lights flashing.

"What the hell?" shouts Ezra. We sprint to the door.

"Enter in the code!" I scream. Ever hurriedly pushes the numbers on the keypad until the door clicks open.

We're not even a foot into the building before we come face to face with a very tall man. He has tan skin and blonde curls, and a devious look in his eyes that would intimidate anyone. "Well, well, well," he speaks, with a very thick German accent. "Platinum, Ever, Hendrix, Alia, Ezra." He props his hands on his hips. "We finally meet."

Before I can even blink, Hendrix yanks out his gun and a tranquilizer bullet pierces the man's leg. He falls on the floor before I get the chance to ask him how he knows my name.

I know it's her the moment I meet her gaze.

She's practically me, but older. The bags under her eyes can't hide their emerald gleam, same as the grey streaks near her roots can't hide her undeniably red hair.

"Jane."

She twirls around instantly, as if she knows it's me who just called her name. I can see the shock swirl in her eyes for a moment, but then it's replaced with a sorrowful remorse.

"Ever."

I don't know how to respond. Do I hug her? Do I hate her for what she did? Of course not, I could never do that. She was just a woman who had so much love for her husband she couldn't bear to live without him.

But instead she ended up here. I'm not sure where the rest of the group ran off to; I gave them my phone so Dreyden could communicate with them. I knew that when I saw the red flash of her ponytail, though, I couldn't walk past my own mother without giving some sort of acknowledgment.

"It's been a while." She says. Her arms are covered with powder and grime. When I look behind her I see jars of dark particles sitting neatly on a shiny black table. She must've been making gun powder for The Forces weaponry.

"Only sixteen years." I smile and choke back tears.

She nods. "You look practically identical to me when I was sixteen. Except you've got Robby's nose. A little bump in the exact same spot, how about that." She laughs a hearty laugh, full of love and goodness.

"Robby," I take a step forward. "Is that my dad?"

I can see the tears fill her eyes as she recalls his memory. "Yes. A very good man, too pure for the hell that is war. When he was drafted—"

"He was drafted?" Now I'm confused. "I thought he chose. I thought it was his choice."

"Goodness, no. Robby was only full of kindness, not a bad bone in his body. He could never shoot a human being, no matter what crimes that human being had committed."

I can't stop the tears from falling. I've never heard about my dad before. Never even knew the slightest bit. Now I feel like I've met him for the first time. "Well, obviously, I didn't get his genes. I'm kind of—"

"A rebel?" My mom smiles at me. "Just like me."

"Yeah." I smirk.

Jane sits down in one of the swivel chairs scattered across the room, and sighs. "What are you doing here, Ever? You never should've come. This is a bad place. Not a place for a girl like you."

I sit down next to her. "I'm here to save you."

"You don't think I've tried saving myself?" She finally breaks down. "I've tried for sixteen years to escape this place. I came here for my husband. I found him. We escaped, but only for a little while. Two months later The Forces found us. He was shot, since his right arm was no good. I was brought back here to work."

"Who do you work with?"

"Soldiers who are still in mildly good condition. They do the manual labor. I used to work with a few other women, wives of some of the soldiers. We'd do the sewing of the uniforms and making of the gunpowder, stuff like that."

I gulp. "What happened to them?"

"I still work with one woman, Avril; as far as I know, though, all the other women are dead. They died from starvation or suicide; we're not treated well here."

I decide to ask the inevitable question. "Why did you leave me?"

"Honey," she bites her lip. "I wasn't in a good place. I was a young woman in love who had no idea what she was doing with her life besides being in love with her husband. I wasn't ready to raise a child, and I knew you'd go somewhere with a better family who could give you a great life."

"I got stuck with a two drug addicts. I practically raised myself!"

She begins to cry. "Ever…"

"Don't." I can't help but storm out of the room, I'm that angry. But quickly, the anger turns to sadness, and I end up leaning against the wall prepared to cry a river.

Until a bullet hits me in the gut.

———

My eyes open to Platinum kneeling over me.

"Are you okay, Ever?" Her tears fall on my face.

The pain isn't as horrible as I thought it would be. It's tolerable, and at least the bleeding has stopped since Platinum wrapped a giant bandage around my entire stomach.

"Thank you," I tell her sincerely. "You saved my life."

She smiles and hoists me up, helping support some of my weight with her arm as she wedges it between my arm pit. "Anything for a friend. But do you know who shot you?"

I shake my head. "I have no idea. He was wrapped all in black, and I didn't have the tranquilizers so I couldn't shoot him. They're probably looking for all of us, though. I mean the alarms went off, it's only a matter of time before we're all shot."

"I guess." She looks down, avoiding my eyes. "Oh, who was that woman with the red hair? She seemed really concerned after you got shot."

I exhale a long, resounding breath. "I don't really know who she is. But I'd like to get to know her."

———

We arrive at a room. This is where we find the others. It's all black, just like all the walls in this torture asylum, but this room's different. There's an entire wall lined with screens of extremely high-tech computers, and another wall holding a large world map with red dots pinned in the majority of the countries. Ezra and Alia are messing with the screens, but Hendrix is studying the map.

I see America's the only country with no pins, except for a green one right in the center.

"What do you think it means?" He looks over at me. "The green dot?"

The jade shade of the small pin only reveals my fear. "Well, red means stop." I pause for a minute. "And green must mean go."

It's only a matter of time.

Those words keep echoing through my head relentlessly. It's only a matter of time before they find us. It's only a matter of time before we're dead.

We learned who the man is, the man who we shot right when we entered. His name is Claus. He runs the German headquarters of The Forces. That's what we read in his file, at least. I don't know how he knows us or what it means, but I'm determined to figure it out.

Ezra and I decided to move this steel desk to see what was behind it, and it revealed a large storage space holding thousands of labeled files of the Awakened, as well as the staff members working here. The only files I couldn't find were ours.

"Guys," Alia spins around from the computer screens she's been monitoring. The look of panic on her face is not reassuring. "The guards are coming." She points at the screen showing the hall outside the room.

I race to the door to make sure that it's locked. "The lock won't be enough, they'll have keys. We need to put something in front of the door so when they open it there will be at least some resistance."

"Already on it." Ezra moves the heavy steel desk. It's fairly heavy, so it should have a good chance of working.

"Ever," Dreyden says through the phone, and we all stop to look at him. "I figured you all would eventually get into a threatening situation like this, so I thought I should tell you. Within the bag of tranquilizers, there's a small loaded gun. If the situation presents itself, you'll be prepared."

One gun isn't going to be enough to save any of us, but it's the thought that counts. "Thank you, Dreyden. We'll make sure to not waste it."

Suddenly, a loud banging comes from the other side of the door.

"Wir wissen, dass ihr da drin seid, macht die Tür auf oder wir schießen!"

"We know you're in there, open up or we'll fire," whispers Alia. "Roughly translated."

Five seconds pass.

They shoot at the lock.

The door explodes open, the frame shattering into hundreds of pieces. Luckily, none of this fazes us too heavily.

"Well, clearly we didn't think that through well enough." Says Ezra.

Claus strides in. He's a little loopy, but otherwise fine.

"You damn Americans," he laughs. "Always thinking you're smarter, cleverer, better." Claus grins a devious smile. "How very wrong you are! This is my house, little Americans. You do not come uninvited. And if you do—" he presses a gun up to Ever's forehead. "I kill you."

"If you pull that trigger on her, I swear on my fucking life I'll pull my trigger on you."

It's a woman with bright red hair. She's holding a gun and pointing it straight at Claus.

"Mom," Ever squeaks. "You don't have to do this."

"That's your Mom?" What the hell? "How come you never told us you found your mother?"

"This isn't the time, Hendrix."

"Well, well, well." Claus releases the gun from Ever's forehead and lets it hang limp by his side. "Jane, I never thought you would turn your back on me. What changed your mind?"

She continues to point her gun at him. "I'll let you treat me like your own doormat, Claus. But I will never let you lay one of your dirty little fingers on my daughter."

"Fine, then. If that's how you want to play, that's how you want to play." Before any of us can even blink, he shoots her in the head.

"Mom!" Ever screams and races to her mother's aid. She's still breathing, but unconscious. "Don't die! Please, don't die!"

Something inside me snaps. "Who raised you? Satan? How could you just shoot a girl's mother like that and not feel an ounce of guilt?"

He looks right at me. "Because you all are the enemy. And no enemy of mine deserves to live." He nods at the guards. "Tie their hands! I do not trust them."

He's about to walk away, but he stares back once more. *"Sie haben fünf Minuten."*

Alia gulps. "We have five minutes."

I'm confused. "Until what?"

"If I were to take a guess, death."

———

"I got it!"

Platinum, Ever and I turn from the map to face them. "What do you mean? What did you get?"

The guards had tied our hands with rope, though Alia could snap it in half with ease. She had then helped us untie our hands, and ran over to work on the equipment.

"Into the system!" Alia yelled. "I tried 9452 just like Dreyden said the entrance code was, and it worked! Come here."

We all rush over to Alia's screen. I check the clock. "We only have two minutes, so hurry."

"The entire army is controlled from these computers. I have their attack plan pulled up on here. They have miniscule cameras attached to the guns in order for the people sitting behind these screens to see through. The humans carrying the guns don't control when or where they shoot, but the people behind these screens do. This way they can get exact measurements through the advanced technology and truly make every shot count. It's genius."

"It's very admirable, but not good for us. How can we possibly shoot all that down within the next sixty seconds?" questions Ezra.

"The coding inscribed is very difficult and specific, but if you guys can hold off the guards long enough I might be able get far enough in to where I can at least shut down some of the weapons. A lot of this is written in German—I can translate the generics but it's going to be a lot more complicated depending on how detailed this is. Plus, it's not just guns, they have everything from electronic devices that emit tear gas to automated bombs. I need time."

"Too late," Claus's voice bounces off the walls behind us. "You're out of time, sweetheart."

And the guns begin to fire.

The first bullet barely misses my arm.

Ezra leaps in front of me, acting as a human shield. He screams as he's hit in the shoulder, and he crumples up like a ragdoll on the floor. He's not as immune to bullets as I am. The characteristics of the Untamed vary, as some are stronger than others.

Every man is for himself. There's probably twenty guards and five of us, but Hendrix, Platinum, and Ever are doing well holding them off by firing back at them with the tranquilizers.

Okay, I need to focus. My friends' lives are at risk.

I first click on the settings for the cameras. If I can deactivate the visibility of the cameras and the ammo stored within the guns, that would be a good start; the primary weaponry for The Forces are guns, after all.

I see a tab labeled "Sight Settings," and a little button pop up next to it; "Turn Off"

I'm not hesitant to press it. Once I do, I see all the cameras shut off. Yes!

"Get the blonde girl!" yells Claus, and points to me. Their bullets come flying in my direction, but only two make contact. I can only feel a pinch, though, and continue to make my way through the files.

Another tab is labeled "Ammunition Settings," and I also gladly click "Turn Off." The tear gas is just as easy to manipulate; when it comes to the bombs, however, it gets trickier.

I have to enter another access code in order to reach the good stuff; the bombs, for example. I tried to enter 9452 again, but it was denied.

Then I realize something.

On all the guards' uniforms, they each have a number. Some have 4, some have 6, some have 0, and some have 2. I bet they have something to do with their ranking, but never mind that; it has to be a combination of those four numbers.

0246. Denied. 6420. Denied. 2064.

Access granted.

I don't even look at what I'm shutting off. I click the deactivate button so many times, my hand starts to hurt. Until I notice everything around me starts to shut off. Something pops up on the computer screen, and when I read it my heart jumps in my throat.

I just shut off the power in the entire building.

It's like I'm immersed into a horror movie. Everything around me turns pitch black, and I'm afraid to move. A gun goes off, and Platinum lets out a short yelp.

"Platinum?" I ask, my voice shaky. "Are you okay?"

No response.

For a second, time has stopped. Nobody moves, and it's so silent you could hear a pin drop. But then the bullets are flying around like lightning bolts striking all at once.

I hear screams from voices I can't make out. It's torture, knowing that my friends might be dying and I haven't a clue. I'm fortunate to be so immune to bullets.

As if someone answered my prayers, the lights flicker back on. I see Claus stride in, a cocky grin plastered to his face. "There's an emergency light switch, darling. Don't act so surprised."

It's then that I finally take in the aftermath around me. Hendrix and Ezra are huddled against the wall, both alive and breathing except for some blood sceping from Ezra's shoulder. Ever is curled up in a fetal position on the floor, uninjured.

But then there's Platinum, sprawled out on the blood-covered tile, unconscious.

I rush to her side. "Platinum? Can you hear me?" I check her neck for a pulse. None.

Regretfully, I glance up at the others. "She's dead."

"No!" Claus shrieks.

What?

"I thought you *wanted* us dead." States Hendrix.

"I'm not talking about the girl; she can go to the guillotine for all I care" He swivels around from his chair. "I'm talking about the system. You shut it down. That's impossible."

"I guess we damn Americans are smarter than you think," sneers Ever.

Claus stands up, and I notice he's shaking. "You kill my army," he murmurs, "I kill you."

"Go!" screams Ezra, and we sprint for the doors. Something burns inside of me, though, something angry. I have to avenge Platinum's death; she did not deserve to die.

I silently creep over to retrieve the pre-loaded gun from the bag of tranquilizers.

"Hey asshole."

Claus turns towards me.

"You kill my friend," I whip out the gun from behind my back, "I kill you."

With one shot to the head, he falls on the floor, and I sprint out of there before the guards have any time to react.

———

I catch up to the others, talking to Ever's mother.

"Come with us, Mom." Ever pleads. "We shut it down, you're safe now! You can be the mother I never had, literally."

Jane shakes her head. She ended up surviving the shot to her head, but barely. "I can't go back, Ever. I've already lost so much; I can't afford to lose anything else. There is someone I'd like you to meet, though, particularly you, Ezra."

A woman walks in, and she's possibly the most beautiful women I've ever seen.

"Kids, meet Avril Callahan, Ezra's biological mother."

Ezra's mouth hangs open. "Mom?"

Avril doesn't even respond; she's crying so hard. She walks up to him and wraps her arms tightly around his body. "I love you so much."

Ezra hugs her back. "I love you too."

A loud hum fades in from what seems like above the roof. Ezra and his mom release their embrace, and we all walk outside

It's a helicopter. "Platinum Woods, Ever Stone, Hendrix Asher, Alia Wordsworth, and Ezra Callahan!" A man's voice booms. "This is the United States Air Force! Hold your hands up and do not move under any circumstances!"

A shock of terror rushes through my veins. "This is it." says Hendrix, and I hold his hand despite the government's orders. I've already broken enough laws, what's one more?

But when the helicopter lands, instead of telling us we're under arrest, a lieutenant steps out and says "Our sincerest appreciation, ladies and gentlemen. You just saved the United States of America."

Today marks five years since we returned from The Forces' headquarters in Germany.

It's so weird to think that was five years ago. I can still remember it like it was yesterday.

"Ez," calls Alia. "Will you watch the twins? I'm going on a run."

A month later she was pregnant with our two little girls, Platinum and Bea. I wasn't so sure about the names to begin with, but Alia insisted.

"It's the least we can do to commemorate them." She had said. Now I love the names, and I wouldn't change them for anything else in the world.

They're the most beautiful little girls in the entire world too. With Alia's golden hair and my pale blue eyes, they resemble a pair of angels.

Alia's about to hand Bea to me when the doorbell rings.

"Did you invite anyone over?"

"No," I shake my head. I still get a little uncomfortable when I'm surprised.

I open the door to find Ever and Dreyden standing on the porch.

"Happy We Saved Our Country Day!" Ever yells, and throws her arms around me. I laugh and hug her back. "Hey, it's been a while!"

Dreyden gives me a friendly nod.

"Hey, Drey, you still tolerating her?"

He laughs and throws an arm around her shoulder. "More or less." Ever and Dreyden are engaged, soon to be married in two months.

The doorbell rings again, and Alia opens it to see Hendrix standing in the doorway.

"Hey, Blondie, I've missed ya."

We all welcome Hendrix inside with open arms. He's been travelling the world with his new job as a journalist. It's perfect for him, considering his appreciation for writing.

We end up sitting on the couches in the living room, discussing normal adult things like how Platinum refuses to eat anything we put on her plate, and how Ever cannot decide on what flowers to use for her wedding bouquets.

"Okay, can we talk about the elephant in the room?" Ever finally declares, folding her arms. "It's been five years, guys. Five years since everything changed for us."

Everything did change when we returned. All the Awakened returned to their families, safe and sound. I still keep in touch with Iris; she lives in a loft in New York, following her dream of being on Broadway. The five of us were awarded medals of Honor, including Platinum, posthumously. They buried it with her in her coffin.

After a few months, though, it was like society had moved on. Nobody recognized us. Nobody realized how much we had sacrificed, at just sixteen years old. It was like everyone wanted to ignore how misleading the government had been, using teenagers as pawns to avoid war. It wasn't right.

"Today isn't about being remorseful, guys." Alia says, and smiles. "Today is about celebrating us. We're *Untamed*. Don't see it as a burden, see it as a blessing."

"A blessing." I grin and kiss her on the cheek. "I like the sound of that."

Alia goes into the kitchen and comes out with five glasses of wine, handing one to each of us. "I want to make a toast. To us, and all the shit that's led us to gather in this room today."

"To us!" Ever and Dreyden raise their glasses.

"To us!" Hendrix follows their lead.

It's at that moment that I realize how much love I have for everyone in this room. We did it. We survived. And now we're thriving more than ever before. I raise my glass as high as I can.

"To us!"

The End

66140514R00156

Made in the USA
Lexington, KY
04 August 2017